Chancers

AMERICAN INDIAN LITERATURE AND CRITICAL STUDIES SERIES

GERALD VIZENOR, GENERAL EDITOR

Also by Gerald Vizenor

FICTION

Hotline Healers: An Almost Browne Novel
Dead Voices: Natural Agonies in the New World
The Heirs of Columbus
Landfill Meditation: Crossblood Stories
The Trickster of Liberty: Tribal Heirs to a Wild Baronage
Griever: An American Monkey King in China
Bearheart: The Heirship Chronicles

NONFICTION

(with A. Robert Lee) *Postindian Conversations*
Fugitive Poses: Native American Indian Scenes of Absence and Presence
Manifest Manners: Narratives on Postindian Survivance
Summer in the Spring: Anishinaabe Lyric Poems and Stories
The People Named the Chippewa

OTHER NARRATIVES

Shadow Distance: A Gerald Vizenor Reader
Interior Landscapes: Autobiographical Myths and Metaphors
Crossbloods: Bone Courts, Bingo, and Other Reports
Earthdivers: Tribal Narratives on Mixed Descent
Wordarrows: Indians and Whites in the New Fur Trade

Chancers

A NOVEL

Gerald Vizenor

UNIVERSITY OF OKLAHOMA PRESS : NORMAN

Chancers is a work of trickster stories and fiction. The names, characters, places, and incidents are either the product of the author's imagination or are used fictitiously, and any resemblance to actual events, cultures, locales, or persons, living, dead, or resurrected, is entirely coincidental.

Library of Congress Cataloging-in-Publication Data

Vizenor, Gerald Robert, 1934–
    Chancers: a novel/Gerald Vizenor.
        p. cm. — (American Indian literature and critical studies series; v. 36)
    ISBN 0-8061-3266-3 (alk. paper)
    1. Phoebe Apperson Hearst Museum of Anthropology—Fiction.
2. Cults—California—Berkeley—Fiction.   3. Indians of North America—
Antiquities—Fiction.   4. Indians of North America—Fiction.
5. Berkeley (Calif.)—Fiction. I. Title. II. Series.

PS3572.I9 C47 2000
813'.54—dc21

                              00-020188

Chancers: A Novel is Volume 36 in the American Indian Literature and Critical Studies Series.

The paper in this book meets the guidelines for permanence and durability of the Committee on Production Guidelines for Book Longevity of the Council on Library Resources, Inc. ∞

1 2 3 4 5 6 7 8 9 10

Slowly he lifts the heavy stones,
a little higher with every sentence,
and there is nothing that can redeem him
except *his own words*.

Elias Canetti, *Notes from Hampstead*

These are futile teasers.
Let them put into my mouth at last
the words that will save me,
damn me, and no more talk about it,
no more talk about anything.

Samuel Beckett, *The Unnamable*

Chancers

SOLAR DANCERS

*The ethnic emissaries
noted in the medical narrative
that his first ecstatic vision
took place on Wednesday,
1 April 1942,
during the full moon
of the fourth month,
four hours before dawn
at the coastal defense bunker
overlooking Rodeo Lagoon
near San Francisco, California.
Saturn, Mars, and Jupiter
were the evening stars.*

TOTEMIC NAMES

Provost Pontius Booker started his short but certain march to the Faculty Club at the University of California. The scent of bay laurel was in the moist air. He paused to admire the arbor, and then a solar dancer touched his shoulder as he crossed the narrow bridge over Strawberry Creek.

Pontius thought nothing of that brush with native fate at the time. Two weeks later he vanished on his routine march to lunch and was never seen again. The university police investigated the situations and then released a rather comic portrait of a sinister man who had been seen near the creek late that morning, but the actual person was a retired historian who was out for a walk with her wolfhound.

Mister Cedar Birdie, said the provost. He turned, cocked his head and beady eyes to the right, and then reached out to shake my hand at the entrance to the Faculty Club.

No, not the birdie.

Forgive me sir, said the provost.

Cedarbird is my name.

Pontius looked away as we crossed over the threshold into the foyer of the Faculty Club. I told him that my nickname was the same as my surname, first and last, one name, but never the diminutive.

I should like to hear more.

Cedarbird, sacred and secular, truly equal in one totemic name. I knew at the time that he was not sincere about my name, but he was there, a captive of his own manifest manners and the tone of my suspensive name story.

Pontius circled the baronial foyer and gestured to his many friends and colleagues. He raised one hand several times, a rather royal wave, wagged two fingers, and then cocked his head slightly to the side. His facile moves were so easy to mock, but no one seemed to notice me at his side. Suddenly, he turned and almost ran me over.

So, what are the stories of *your* names?

Nothing quite so sacred, said the provost. My names are of history. He smiled, waved to another colleague, then cocked his head once more and moved away. His eyes were cold, blue, and beady, but his herringbone twill shirt had a warm tone. My moment was at hand when he turned his back to me a second time.

Provost, forgive me, what is that mark?

Pontius pretended to hear my question, as he had the stories of my name, but then, as we passed a mirror in the foyer, he turned to see a bright blue character on the shoulder of his sports coat.

Whatever could it be?

Blue chalk?

Doubtless, said the provost. He brushed his shoulder and the blue character created a numinous, winter haze in the foyer. Several faculty members on their way to lunch paused to comment on the marvelous, shimmering ruins of the character.

Some obscure monogram, said the provost.

Audacious graffito, said a medievalist.

Quite a labyrinth, said a political scientist.

Clearly, the trace of the character is the figure of a shaman, observed a cultural anthropologist. Two historians brushed their shoulders and teased the provost about certain academic shamans on the campus. Boldly, the director of art practices announced that the image was faux primitive, the actual creation of a modern artist. The numinous haze turned our shadows blue in the mirror.

The director of postethnic studies on the campus considered the character and declared that it was calligraphy. Clearly

Chinese, he said, and then traced the dusty strokes with one finger.

Nonsense, said the provost.

What does it mean?

Dead, *se*, or to die, said the director.

Really?

Yes, and *dai*, the four stroke common radical of the character, means bad or evil, and that, you see, combines with other radicals to mean cruel and death, said the director. He moved back with his hand over his heart.

Blackboard shamans, said the anthropologist.

Hardly, said the provost, a linguist and philosopher who had not lectured in a classroom for more than a decade. Naturally, he was distracted more by the comments of the faculty than by the mysterious character on his sports coat.

Cedarbird, are you the shaman?

Clearly, you need one.

Hocuspocus, said the provost.

The touch of a *wiindigoo*.

Touch of what?

The *wiindigoo*, a cannibal monster.

Really, said the provost.

That blue winter haze around you might be the very breath of the *wiindigoo* teasers. You might have been touched by the flesh eaters, and you should see a shaman right away.

Naturally, said the provost.

Truly, see a protective shaman.

The provost became a victim of his own rational repudiation of native shamans, naive realism, and tricky stories.

Strangely, in an obscure reversal of academic fortunes, he embraced a poseur over an erotic round dancer, a rogue over a great storier.

Pardone de Cozener was the poseur, a stinky man who mocked natives and lectured on tribal law, casino politics, and sovereignty. Cozzie White Mouth, as he was known to the solar dancers, always wore feathers, stained chicken feathers, braided in his hair and tied like ribbons to his sleeves. He owned a chicken pluck center on the side and shared a small storefront near campus with the noted transvestite, Mannie Medicine.

De Cozener actually convinced the provost to declare an academic reservation in People's Park on a remote section of university land, and then he petitioned the federal government to open a casino in the name of Ishi, the very first native to work for the University of California. Cozzie lost favor with the solar dancers, a ruck of outlaw students, when he boldly proposed that a museum be established at the casino to display the skeletal remains of natives and the preserved brain of Ishi. He had the good ear of the provost, but not for long, because the *wiindigoo* solar dancers had the actual head and heart of the provost that semester.

Peter Roses, my faculty mentor, was the director of native studies on the campus. He was a great lecturer, and very active with blondes, the natural enemies of the poseurs. Mostly, his humor and sense of irony caught the enmity of every romantic native student on campus. Roses would not stand for even the slightest pout or plea of victimry.

De Cozener had an overactive alimentary canal and constantly farted. He was always alone on elevators, and only the naive rode with him in a car. The mystery, as you know, was how a man with stout, tight cheeks could break so much air without a sound. The secretary in native studies said he farted out of his mouth. Maybe so, but he practiced a crucial reach in the right direction to avoid a fleshy vibration. He was isolated as much by intestinal gas as he was by a conspiratorial association with the solar dancers, those students who were possessed by the outrage of *wiindigoo* stories. The solar dancers hated the round dancers, the many blondes who had sex with my mentor, and the native students who refused to separate their minds from the erotic. Roses was the natural partisan of the round dancers, and the solar dancers resented his survivance stories and carnal play.

Pontius turned, cocked his head once more, and hurried down the hardwood corridor to a lunch conference in the Clyde Kluckhohn Courtyard. He passed the framed portraits of previous provosts mounted on both sides of the passage. They leaned out of their academic poses and, with practiced, totemic smiles, touched their colleagues on the way. That corridor was the eternal reign of academic villainy.

Pontius Booker vanished two weeks later on his wonted march, late in the day, to the Faculty Club. The police reported four giant footprints in the area and observed traces of blood in the log cabin on campus, but nothing more. He was the first to lose his head to the *wiindigoo* solar dancers that summer at the University of California. The practiced smile of the provost was pictured in many news stories around the world, but he shared that imagic moment with the comic portrait of a likely perpetrator.

ETHNIC EMISSARIES

I had written that much, line for line as you read it now, when three *wiindigoo* solar dancers, otherwise students in native studies, cornered me in the computer encryption center on campus. The solar dancers were on one of their ceremonial meanders and demanded to know what brought me to a computer terminal so late at night. The *wiindigoo* are winter monsters and cannibals in *anishinaabe* stories, but the new *wiindigoo* haunted the campus as native students and solar dancers. They were possessed by the ideologies of victimry.

I should have told them, then and there, as another scene was transmitted to the ethnic emissaries and my editors, that I was not only a native lecturer, but a novelist, a native prosateur, and a secret agent. I told them almost that much, but rather as a strategic tease in the trickster manner of stories. I was not worried, at the time, because they were terminal creeders, morose separatists, and four directionists, and not one of them had ever listened to my lectures or stories in the past. They would never read my stories.

These scenes are read by my ethnic emissaries as intelligencer reports, and the very same scenes are read as stories by my editors at Random Nation Books. Both companies, as you know, are private. The emissaries have no name or location, a virtual, private intelligence agency with a computer presence but no trace of a past. They would agree, but they seldom write to me. The emissaries are an absence, and, much like native tricksters, they exist only in the virtual instance of their stories.

My scenes and stories are presented just once as an encrypted electronic narrative. The ethnic emissaries use my scenes to create extended narratives for thousands of subscribers in private corporations and in many government agencies around the world. There is an urgent need for more intelligence since the incredible cast of casinos and the rise of native claims against governments over the many violations of nineteenth century treaties.

The most distinguished explorers and missionaries did as much in the past, but their stories became historical documents. Matteo Ricci, Christopher Columbus, Lewis and Clark, Theodore Roosevelt, and Claude Lévi-Strauss were intelligencers and ethnic emissaries. Everyone, you see, has some need for esoteric stories about natives, some need to gather ethnic secrets on the other. Many of my scenes, as you know, are used by lawyers, teachers, politicians, university administrators, police, and by various state and federal agencies.

The ethnic emissaries and my editors were the very first to learn about the *wiindigoo* solar dancers, the provost, and the other faculty and administrators who were sacrificed and beheaded that spring at the University of California.

The emissaries and my editors could be the same readers, for that matter, but who would know? My stories describe the actual events of the solar dancers on the campus, but my best scenes are imagic situations, created to convince the emissaries and editors that my memories are true, conscientious, and worth the advance royalties.

My actual memories are secrets, even in these scenes and stories. Secrets are my ontic sense of presence, my true connections to the nature of others. My sense of the sacred is secret, and secrets are much closer to creation than authority, sacrifice, moral liturgy, or victimry. Political causes are separations, the absence of the sacred, as you know, and the most obvious liturgies are nothing more than sandwich boards worn by those natives who are lost in the burdens of the past and the future of victimry.

My secrets create a sense of presence, and my stories are mythic connections, not separations. Secrecy is sacred, and the very reason for trickster stories. Novelists are visionaries, and, because our secrets are considered dangerous to the consumers of native cultures and to the rogues of pride and promises, we are the outsiders, the shamans, the shunters of tradition in the community. My stories are a real and tricky presence, a native contradiction, a shamanic apologue, but never a separation. Those who are run by mean manners and traditions are the separatists.

The three solar dancers who discovered me in the computer center waited for an explanation. I told them that my stories were secrets, the scenes of a novelist and ethnic espionage agent. First they stared at me, then teased me, but they would not believe my obvious story.

Consider me a trickster with a computer, a trickster in the best tradition of transformation, and a secret agent for a virtual ethnic intelligence agency. My stories are sold to many universities, including this one, and, of course, to every government agency that has anything to do with natives. The solar dancers heard me say that, word for word, in a tricky, secretive tone of voice. My gestures count with the separatists, but the tricky tone of my voice means nothing to the emissaries. The three listened in silence and then, in close order, shouted

at me. Their shouts were more a native tease than an accusa-
tion of treason or treachery.

What secrets?

Man, what is this shit?

Fucking trickster?

I printed their *wiindigoo* nicknames, their actual solar dance
names, and each blunt tease on the computer display monitor
by Touch Tone, Fast Food, and Token White. Bad Mouth, her
brother Knee High, Injun Time, and Fine Print luckily were
not there. The solar dancers were a ruck of cultural fusions,
crude revisions, and naive sanguinity. I then entered a secret
code, the one that connected me to my editor, and brought to
the screen the first scene of my stories:

*Provost Pontius Booker started his short but certain march to the
Faculty Club at the University of California. The scent of bay laurel
was in the moist air. He paused to admire the arbor, and then a solar
dancer touched his shoulder as he crossed the narrow bridge over
Strawberry Creek.*

Shit, you were there, said Touch Tone.

The birdie man, said Fast Food.

My Mojave bow, said Token White.

The *wiindigoo* blues, said Touch Tone.

My stories are satirical, as you know, and sometimes my
editors pretend they are lost in the ironies and word play. The
emissaries once raised doubts about the facts, accuracy, and
authenticity of my stories. Satire, they soon learned, was far
more authentic than any romance or literal historical narratives.

I invited my editors and the ethnic emissaries to consider
the natural, most obvious satire in stories about native casinos.

How could the reversal and contradiction of winners and losers on a reservation not be a satire? What native traditions are worth the venture of losers, the compulsive, bored senior citizens at casinos? Native sovereignty ends over a slot machine. The same is true of every romantic notion about natives. Start with the name *indian*, the occidental invention of the *indian*, the *nominis umbra*, or the shadow name that has no substance, and you have five centuries of satire in one causal, common noun. So, in the real case of the native solar dancers, the *wiindigoo*, and the beheaded provost, satire is the true mode of espionage, an authentic trickster story.

I wrote to the emissaries that my satire was not a romance of shame, never harsh, social ridicule, but a mythic connection to native oral stories and the remains of our ancestors. Robert Elliott writes in *The Power of Satire* about a "mystical ethos," and that ethos might be seen in some native ceremonies and understood in the tease of trickster stories. My stories to the ethnic emissaries were a natural tease, the mythic satires of native chancers in the new word wars.

Once the emissaries understood that *indians* were the marvelous inventions of colonists, missionaries, spies, and social scientists, my stories were accepted as intelligence. In fact the emissaries increased the payments for my stories in only a few months. They gathered scenes from other sources, some more archival than mine, and at times sent me the secured narratives. My solar dance scenes were augmented in that way.

The ethnic emissaries were never traceable. Every message was the last one, and one last message to me was surprisingly ironic, a quotation from *Mythologies* by Roland Barthes. "Myth hides nothing and flaunts nothing: it distorts; myth is neither a lie nor a confession: it is an inflexion." Myth "transforms history into nature," and "it is not read as a motive, but as a reason."

So, native myths are not the motive by natural reason, and my stories are the satire of a *wiindigoo* sacrifice on campus. Secrets are my very nature, my chancer nature, and the mythic scenes in my stories are virtual satires.

The emissaries asked me several times if the provost had actually been sacrificed, and if a real crime had been committed. Yes, of course, was my response, but the question should have been, How did you create the scenes and stories of such an eerie crime?

Pontius was beheaded that spring semester, the learned scapegoat of a gruesome atonement. The provost and the others were the sacrifice of native praise, the savage possession of an unearthly *wiindigoo*, and with each consecration a native chancer was resurrected in the blood, bones, and names of the provostry.

Pontius was the start, and the solar dancers marked several more victims that semester with blue scapegoat characters. Some were marked in the arbor near the creek and sacrificed in a log cabin behind the Faculty Club. Others were beheaded and dissected in the museum. The sacrifices were precise, only those lecturers, professors, scientists, and administrators who were associated with the abuse and misuse of the thousands of native bones and chancers stored in the Phoebe Apperson Hearst Museum of Anthropology at the University of California.

The native chancers are ecstatic visions, the memories of an imagic presence, and by their museum bones the chancers await resurrection in person, spirit, and stories. There are shamans who trace the stories of the native chancers and create a wild sense of presence, a mighty *mikawi* survivance or return to consciousness.

"The violation of burial sites and the confiscation of human remains have been shameful and unprofessional," wrote N. Scott Momaday in the *New York Times*. His editorial essay considered the separation of native creationists and evolutionists over the skeleton of Kennewick Man. "Wounds to the spirit are considered eminently more serious than wounds to the body."

Still, the ethnic emissaries insisted on more evidence, the material facts to document my stories. The provost and others were sacrificed, and without a trace of their heads, or any other body parts for that matter. Clearly, the absence of their heads was both evidence and satire. The only direct connections to the sacrifices were the resurrection of native remains, the grave return of the chancers. The absence of one created the actual presence of the other.

Samuel Beckett came to mind many times in my reports to the ethnic emissaries. "Words and images run riot in my head, pursuing, flying, clashing, merging, endlessly," he wrote in *Malone Dies*. "But beyond this tumult there is a great calm, and a great indifference, never really to be troubled by anything again."

FOUR SKINS

Natives were the chancers of their visions and names. Some names were sacred, some were borrowed, dreamed, stolen, and the nicknames of survivance were totemic stories. Descriptive names in translation were more of manner than chance, more document than tricky, and a greater distance to native visions and stories.

Traditional natives lost a great secret when they revealed their sacred names to missionaries, and that was the very start of ethnic espionage. The name games have never been the same since the translation of sacred names. Today, the word wars over names are ironic, as natives assume bird and animal names to tease a trace of tradition and to reverse the absence of nicknames and survivance stories.

My other names, the actual entries on my birth certificate, have become my secret names, an ironic, secular reversal of traditional native names. My editors and the ethnic emissaries have never seen my archive names. They know me only by my descriptive bird name, my best disguise in the word wars of authenticity.

Ruby Blue Welcome, a Creek and Seminole crossblood, was a senior lecturer on native religions. Ruby was a precious, descriptive name for the birthmark on her throat, a translucent stone. Blue Welcome was translated by missionaries as a surname, a native vision of the mighty blue healers, but she was far, far from any tricky, imagic moments in the stories of her name. She wore no disguise by names.

The provost, aroused by the birthmark and the sound of her metaphoric names, appointed her the director of native admissions. So, by native names we were distinctive, but we had arrived at the academic turnstile with the same stories as the students, invented by discovery, removal, and reservations, and forever a translation of absence. Sadly, many bright native students became the very aliens of their own stories of victimry.

My scenes and stories are about the others who created new visions and names in the cities, a tricky sense of native presence and survivance. The sacred was a secret, but who could ever name the sacred of native traditions? The sacred was in the story. Then and now was just another story, not the sacred measure of time. The native chancers were traces of survivance in stories.

Blue Welcome was the satire not the source of sacred stories, because too soon she was separated by names, numbers, manners, and scores. She posed with the abusers of native chancers, praised the historical archives of dominance, and honored theories over intuition, dreams, and personal experiences. She was ruled by grammars, not by the sacred stories of mighty *blue welcome* healers, not by the colors of summer on the river, the presence of the otter woman, or the blue resurrection of native chancers. She might have been a church organist, but instead became part political scientist, part faux feminist, and a very strange expert on the lexical loot of the Sun Dance Religion.

She was always an uninvited speaker at protests for student control of courses in the department. Truly, uninvited speakers were never a surprise at native events, but some speakers were more insecure and uninvited than others. Blue Welcome was never invited to anything. The solar dancers, in fact, tried to trick her out of their protests, but she was always there, and forever uninvited.

Blue Welcome was moved by her mouth, a natural demise, and every morning she practiced tricky pouts and mouth beams in the mirror. She had no idea that every uninvited

word was one closer to her last on the campus. Most native
students were hardly dedicated to anything academic, but
they were absolutely determined to remove her as a lecturer
and director of admissions. Protest by protest, her uninvited
stories became the history of how and why she lost her head
that semester.

The solar dancers protested to the provost that she punished real natives with low grades, that she was not interested
or active in the community, and that she failed to advance
their separatist causes and courses. They demanded that she
be removed as a lecturer and director of admissions. The
provost disregarded their protest and encouraged the solar
dancers to take remedial courses in the summer.

She raised the microphone to her enormous mouth with
one hand and frowned in the bright sunlight. Once more she
rushed the student protest on Sproul Plaza. She wore a cerise
suit and tight sandals, so tight that her giant brown toes
reached out and touched the concrete. She told the student
audience to watch her right hand, a signature invitation, which
was hidden under a small blue and red blanket.

Four Skins, her trusty hand puppet, waited to be heard, but
not by the solar dancers. Most of the native students were
bored by the intrusive puppet and his tiresome stories. The
other students on the plaza, however, had never seen or heard
the little man with a giant penis in the hands of Blue Welcome.

Let it never be forgotten, or forgiven, students and friends,
that there is the sure hand of a woman directing the move-
ments of his dumb feathered head, she shouted into the microphone. The native students scorned her presence and stories.

Blue Welcome boomed, hissed, and whistled, and her voice pitched and bounced on the concrete in Sproul Plaza. The leaves on the fists of sycamores shivered over her stories. The students had permission to use the microphone for one hour, a university strategy to control events on the plaza. Blue Welcome had encroached on the protest, and the students shouted that she was never, never, never welcome in any color. That, of course, was just what the protest needed to attract a wild audience.

Blue Welcome shouted dumb, dumb, dumb, and that was her own cue to raise the red and blue blanket. Naturally, the audience thought she was shouting at the students, but instead she uncovered a brightly painted tribal hand puppet with a warrior headdress made of sparrow feathers.

Four Skins is his sacred name, she told the audience. She moved his head, leatherbound arms, and comical oversized plastic hands. The ceremonial puppet opened his wide mouth and blinked several times. The audience burst into laughter at the sight of thunderbirds painted on his huge plastic eyelids. Once more, the solar dancers had lost the protest to that impertinent puppet.

Four Skins is the minimal tribal man, the little man with no woman in him but these three fingers, shouted Blue Welcome. See how his big mouth moves, crowing with bad grammar, just like a man. Then, when she removed her fingers from the puppet his head went limp and dropped forward, reversing the drape of his headdress. This little man speaks for the last of the noble savages, but we are in the new world now and tribal women rule, she shouted into the microphone. Once more she thrust her hand into his head, and the native men shouted right back, of course, but soon realized that they had lost the audience to a hand puppet.

Tribal women would never invent a feathered man to mimic as a hunter, but the whiteman did just that, said Blue Welcome. The hunted, perhaps, but not the hunter. She raised her voice to chant, but the sound was closer to a hissy warble. Remember, women never canted their medicine secrets, and they never trapped animals for stupid felt hats. Tribal women are the sacred bears, bison, and vision birds now, and we gather berries with our bare hands, not with bad dreams about animals. We touch what we eat and return the seeds to the earth. Men turn the water sour with their bad dreams and filthy habits with animals.

Bury your mouth, shouted Bad Mouth.

Hands too, mocked Knee High.

Someone shouted a mock war cry.

Blue Welcome moved her chin from side to side and warbled into the microphone. Four Skins, she asked, what ever happened to General George Armstrong Custer at the Little Big Horn?

Custer caught it, said Four Skins.

Caught what?

Custer caught clap from a shepherd, said the puppet as he mimicked her chin moves. He got it from a mule who got it from a mule skinner who got it from a sheep who got it from a shepherd who got it from his mother.

Never mind, said Blue Welcome.

He lost that too, said Four Skins.

Four Skins nodded his plastic head, lowered his chin, opened his pink mouth, and waited for another question. He pretended to be surprised when she raised his breechclout. Right there on the plaza she exposed his bright beaded moccasins and enormous brown penis.

Give that puppet a condom, shouted a student.

Most of the students in the audience had lost interest in the puppet by the time the microphone was disconnected at the end of the hour. The students moved across the plaza to participate in a condom inflation race sponsored by three fraternities. Join the rubber race and condom revolution, several students shouted as they raised bouquets of condom balloons.

Mannie Medicine, the noted transvestite healer, was on the plaza to promote his inflatable blondes for overnight service. He had several blondes at his side, some were stretched and tumid and the others floating on a line with the condoms. My blondes are secure sex, said Mannie. Four Skins, however, caught his eye, as you know, and he decided to create a better blonde as a hand puppet.

Near Sather Gate, a man decorated with black polka dots was towing a green garden hose. Three guitarists, a drummer, a show tune singer in a sombrero, a nasty band of student communists in red berets, a fire eater in a morning coat, a man who bestowed miniature orange trees, two evangelists, one in a postal uniform, and assorted crazies of love and hate were in competition for the same audience on the plaza.

The Hiawatha Confessions, a popular shriving booth and peep show near the fountain on the plaza, was another target of the solar dancers. The sides of the booth were decorated with

three giant portraits. Hiawatha, the Onondaga leader who created the Iroquois Confederacy, was on the back, Minnehaha,
the fantastic native lady of laughing waters, was on one side,
and on the other, the ironist Henry Wadsworth Longfellow.
Hiawatha and Minnehaha faded naturally in the midday sun,
but the poet bore more than a hundred scars from arrows,
knives, and cigarette burns. Longfellow was scalped at least
twice a week in fair weather.

Lama Ho and two lecturers in American Studies established
the campus confessional for money and the stories. The three
opened a food booth on wheels, but their eclectic cuisine and
edible menus did not survive the hardy midday competition,
so they converted the booth to a coin-operated theme confessional and peep show on animals. They mounted a parking
meter at the entrance and wired the booth with a voice activated recorder. Confessions were teased and recorded, and a
wide range of animal sex scenes were presented on peep show
videos for a quarter a minute. The booth earned a few dollars
a day, mostly from curious tourists, but then animal sex
became an issue on the campus and their prurient profits
soared.

Provost Pontius Booker unwittingly turned a very mar-
ginal operation on wheels into a gold mine when he ordered
the university police to seize the pornographic animal peep
show. "Provost Grabs Sexy Animals" was the first banner
headline, and the campus newspaper ran variations of the
story for several weeks. The animal scenes were reviewed by
lawyers and several faculty and student committees. Finally,
the chancellor apologized for the overreaction to explicit

beastly passions when animal rights activists protested every scientific laboratory on the campus. Science is obscene, animals are clean, shouted the activists. Close the laboratories, not the peep shows.

Tulip Browne, the native private investigator, and her niece Conk, who had just been hired to teach a dreamy course on visionary sovereignty in native studies, waited in line to enter the Hiawatha Confessions.

Who's in there? asked Conk.

Nobody, said Tulip.

Who listens to confessions?

Nobody, said Tulip.

What are we waiting for then? asked Conk.

Nothing but the money.

Conk Browne pushed the heavy black velvet curtains aside and they entered the booth. The interior was dusky. The dark walls were decorated with sepia pictures of natives. Tulip inserted four quarters in the parking meter and waited for instructions. The names of various animals blinked on the panel, but she touched the button for confessions and activated a resonant voice that read from *The Song of Hiawatha* by Henry Wadsworth Longfellow.

> *By the shore of Gitche Gumee,*
> *By the shining Big-Sea-Water,*
> *At the doorway of his wigwam,*
> *In the pleasant Summer morning,*
> *Hiawatha stood and waited,*
> *What is your confession today?*

Whose voice was that? asked Conk.

N. Scott Momaday, said Tulip.

No, but he sounds almost the same, said Conk. She told me they pretended their confessions in four minutes, and had no idea why. Maybe it was the anonymity, the contradiction of privacy in a public place, and the actual sounds of so many people around the booth. Conk avowed that she had rescued the bones of her sister, Pocahontas, at a secret grave site near Indian Queens in Cornwall. Tulip was shriven by the investigative stories she told about the wiles of men and their perversions. The time on the meter expired with six lines from *The Song of Hiawatha.*

> *Let us welcome, then, the strangers,*
> *Hail them as our friends and brothers,*
> *And the heart's right hand of friendship*
> *Give them when they come to see us.*
> *Gitche Manito, the Mighty,*
> *Said this to me in my vision.*

Blue Welcome set out to lecture on male dominance and mother earth memories at a historical conference a month or so later, but the audience insisted on a few words from her fine feathered warrior in the breechclout.

Four Skins, Four Skins, the historians shouted as she started her lecture. Once more she was humiliated by men, native men, but she would never turn away from a microphone and an audience.

Blue Welcome shifted her chin from side to side, pulled the puppet out of her shoulder holster, thrust her hand into his slack head, and fingered him into position. She touched his cold plastic nose to her cheek. Four Skins, she told the historians, was her very best friend in the world.

Historians, some might say, are not easy to amuse, especially in large numbers at a conference, but a native hand puppet with a giant dick had them in stitches.

General Custer and his various demises were easy humor at native conferences, but the ventriloquy stories of his venereal disease strained the moment. She heard the silence, for once, and asked the puppet another question about white warriors in tight trousers, but the audience was more interested in her marvelous, mythic connections to the puppet than in the actual projection of her voice and stories.

Blue Welcome and her cheeky puppet were marked with blue characters and sacrificed later that semester. Four Skins, however, did not vanish without a trace. His brown penis was discovered in a display case at the Phoebe Apperson Hearst Museum of Anthropology.

BUNKER VISIONS

The San Francisco Solar Dancers, a ruck of urban warriors moved by the *wiindigoo* cannibal, created their own demonic ceremonies and totemic nicknames. They carried raccoon medicine pouches packed with wing bones, feathers, vitamins, cedar punk, sunstones, and sage. For months the solar dancers cursed and conspired to resurrect native chancers and remove Four Skins.

Shit, man, send that plastic geek on permanent relocation somewhere, shouted Bad Mouth. She was a Miwok and Bedouin crossblood who had earned the most obvious nickname of any native on the campus, and her curses ran straight to the bone. Bad Mouth was a *wiindigoo* solar dancer of uncommon horrors.

Man, plastic geek, said her tetchy brother Knee High. He was always perched right behind his sister, and he mocked her hisses and sneers. On his own he warbled at protests and practiced a rather hokey *indian* hand talk that nobody could understand.

Sergeant Cloud Burst, the maniacal, sunstruck veteran of the Second World War, envisioned the San Francisco Solar Dancers. He traced his unnamed native ancestors to a sepia photograph. That imagic connection became a curse of native coincidence, because his visions, solar torments, and *wiindigoo* execrations captured the imagination and spirit of seven lost, lonesome, and desperate students on campus.

Bad Mouth was the actual mouthpiece of this coincidence, and the students were dominated by her vile curses. That thick, incredible consonance of cultural torments, dangerous visions, resentments, and low grades in required courses conjured the wicked *wiindigoo*, the cannibal monsters of *anishinaabe* stories. These students of animus and native rage became the new *wiindigoo* of the concrete, the ominous simulars of tradition who sacrificed the thieves and academic abusers of native bones.

The ethnic emissaries teased these scenes with stories about vampires. The solar dancers, in a sense, were the mutant vampires of a secular, native separation in the city. You could say that the stories of the *wiindigoo* are the consequences of five centuries of abuse and cultural dominance. The hatred, you see, was a blood feud that may never end. The native students, it seems to me, have their own fears of being devoured by giants, the academic *wiindigoo* on campus. So, the antidote was to become a solar dancer and devour the evil enemy. The stories were one thing, but the actual abduction and dissection of the faculty was another.

George Nelson, the early nineteenth century fur trader, mentioned the *wiindigoo* in his published journal, *The Orders of the Dreamed*. He wrote that the giant was a winter creature who devoured certain natives and haunted many others in their dreams. "These Giants as far as I can learn reside somewhere about the *North Pole;* and even at this day frequently pay their unwelcome visits, but which, however, are attended with a complete fright only. It seems also that they delegate their Power to the indians occasionally; and *this* occasions that cannibalism which is Produced, or proceeds rather from a sort of distemper much resembling *maniaism*."

Blue Welcome was resented and cursed by the solar dancers more than anyone on campus. The cruel irony, now that she is gone, is that she actually supported the special admission of the very native students who hated her the most. Knee High, for instance, could barely read a newspaper, and yet he charmed the director of admissions with his crude hand talks. Blue Welcome said he had the hands of a native puppet master.

Bad Mouth and her brother were racial separatists, a radical pose that had no native origins. They divided the earth
into four absolute directions. Cloud Burst and the solar dancers
cursed prime numbers and tediously created an unnatural
world of seasons, memories, ceremonies, directions, and stories in severe combinations of the fundamental fours. Token
White was the eighth and last *wiindigoo*, the blonde who saved
the solar dancers from a prime number. She was always
dressed in black, a tribute to Johnny Cash.

The more creative spiritualists, on the other hand, begot a
universe of seven sides. The four directions, of course, and the
earth, the solar rise of creation, and the native storier at the center.

Bad Mouth would not graduate because she had failed a
basic course on the Sun Dance Religion. Blue Welcome, in turn,
would not waive the grade, and that, to many native students,
was the reason she was beheaded that semester. Actually, she
loved an osteologist and protected his scientific abuse of
native remains. The solar dancers severed her head to resurrect a native chancer.

The San Francisco Solar Dancers were natives of resentments and malice, and each one of them sought their wicked
visions in the cold bunkers, corners, and containers of the city.
They were the solar dancers of the concrete. Cloud Burst and
his *wiindigoo* ruck wore dark clothes, silver buckles, lapis
lazuli, and turquoise rings, and they beat the blue character on
the drum fiercely.

Bad Mouth was moved by Antonin Artaud and the Theatre
of Cruelty. She acted out his miserable simulation of natives
and erotic wars of the senses. The Tarahumara, he wrote,

believe that those who live in cities are mistaken, but that notion became an ironic virtue to Bad Mouth. Artaud, the surrealist, and Bad Mouth, the solar dancer, wanted violence to come alive and words to hurt as much as wounds. One must be "made of the same substance as nature," he wrote in *The Peyote Dance*, not merely close to the words of nature. The Tarahumara once derived their "magical powers from the contempt they have for civilization."

Bad Mouth and the others were the *wiindigoo* of the concrete, the solar dancers of malice, the natives of a turgid consciousness who had returned to atavistic senses and the violence of nature in the city. The *wiindigoo* medicine pouches were varmint raccoons that had been poisoned by an exterminator.

My world is of the word, as you know, and not the wounds of nature, but the ethnic emissaries wanted to know more about the actual, gruesome details of the crimes, and how the *wiindigoo* solar dancers created their own Theatre of Cruelty at the University of California.

Sergeant Cloud Burst, conjuror of the San Francisco Solar Dancers, the curious steward of sinister traditions and vendor of name ceremonies in the city, cupped his right ear in the tribal manner and beat the ceremonial character on the drum, the same character that marked the shoulder of the provost. He wailed in ritual pain for the wounds of his native nature and memories. The sound of his pained voice chased insects, wilted leaves, and teased domestic birds out of flight.

Cloud Burst and his ruck of solar dancers beat the drum four times a week on Sproul Plaza. Bad Mouth and her brother Knee High, Fast Food, Touch Tone, Injun Time, Fine Print, and

Token White answered his natural wail, his somber beck and call at the drum. The solar dancers were the last great wailers of native miseries and the new eerie moan of cultural torment and cruelty in the city.

Fast Food, Athabaskan and Russian crossblood, was a student of the fur trade. He was an awkward dancer with enormous white feet, and he smoked thin black cigars.

Touch Tone, Lakota and Hindustani crossblood, was a student of shamanism and meditative incense. She was stout and wore muted, loose clothes decorated with many ribbons. Each ribbon, she said, was a tribute to Louis Riel, a distant native relative who was sentenced to death for treason.

Injun Time, Lumbee and others, was a student of federal law and shakers. He was an ecstatic dancer, always wore exceptional white clothes, and conducted peculiar marriage ceremonies on campus.

Fine Print, Cherokee and Chinese crossblood, was a student of linguistics, calligraphy, ancient archery, and an advocate of animal liberation, but he was not good at anything. He strongly protested the use of animals in research on campus, but at the same time he tortured domestic cats.

Token White, German and Norwegian crossblood, the only blonde in the ruck of solar dancers, was an expert on native bows and arrows. She carried a decorated quiver over one shoulder, a portable compact disc player over the other, and was obsessed with the music of Johnny Cash.

I Walk the Line. . . .

The solar dancers were the marvelous, malevolent others, estranged crossbloods with no more than resentments and ritual torments in common. The tolerance of their union was situational, and their course was revised by lust, fear, suspicion, abandon, and tricky experiences. Bad Mouth and Knee High were related, but the other solar dancers had only the myth of the cosmic *indian* to bestow in stories. Token White and Fine Print, however, shared a passion for archery. She was an expert on native bows and arrows, as you know, and he was a student of archery in China. Fine Print strained to create a fusion of cultures in bows and arrows, Cherokee and Chinese. He was an eclectic poseur, not a meditative archer, and his showy, reckless manner would be his ruin.

The mere sound of those cloud clowns brings on foul weather, said Peter Roses, an Osage and Portuguese crossblood, and one of the most popular lecturers on campus. Play is a form of extreme punishment to those poseurs, and laughter is an absolute curse. Listen to that thunder, the worst of the urban contraries, the very heart of cultural darkness, and everyone of them, right down to their dyed braids and plastic bear claws, would rather be blonde. Cloud Burst, more than anyone, is a mundane simulation and the natural host of victimry.

Roses was my faculty mentor, an essayist and short story writer, and he was otherwise known to most students on campus as Round Dance. By magic, he could tease a woman into sex and then boast of her conquest. Round Dance was an ironic nickname that described his lecture moves in the center of the classroom. The oral tradition was the last of the great erotic arts, he told me many, many times.

We were standing in the shade under the sycamores on the plaza when a blonde, an explicit dancer, pranced and pirouetted through the dark wail of the solar dancers and the thunder of their drum. She was a sunbeam, and with each sensuous turn to the wild beat she unbuttoned her blouse and flashed her perfect white breasts to the crowd.

Cloud Burst beat the character on the drum harder, thunder in every fierce thrust, and the pitch of his wail cut conversations, scared the sparrows, and mocked the insects. The leaves trembled and wilted on the sycamores. The blonde circled the drum several times and tormented the severe singers and dancers.

Listen, white bitch, this is a sacred song, and no bare tits are allowed near the drum, said Bad Mouth. The outsider smiled and continued to dance around the *wiindigoo* drum, and on the fourth circle the blonde removed the rest of her clothes. The pleasures of nature and solar dance miseries were at war on the plaza.

White bitch, screamed Knee High.

Sacred time, said Injun Time.

Token White, the only blonde solar dancer, moved to the side and concentrated on the moves of the nude blonde as she circled the solar drum. Her narrow white feet barely touched the concrete as she danced.

Token White steadied her breath, a natural meditation that transcended the sound and motion on the plaza, braced her short, curved Apache bow made from a white hickory wagon wheel hoop, and nocked a hazel branch arrow trimmed with three bright woodpecker feathers. She aimed the hand-flaked obsidian point of the arrow right at the bare breasts of the blonde dancer.

Round Dance reached out to the nude blonde on the last turn and guided her gently to the shade of the sycamores. She pirouetted several times in the shadows. He admired her generous moves and was aroused by the thick blond hair on her arms and legs. She wore a bright tattoo of a hummingbird on her shoulder. Round Dance told her the tattoo was enough to be native, and her golden body hair was enough to pass his course.

Token White slowly lowered the bow and stowed the arrow in her otter skin quiver. Only then did she notice the hummingbird and smile at the blonde, a conversion of attitude and spirit. Slowly, she returned to the gloom of the solar dance circle.

Pardone de Cozener moved closer, and his chicken feathers bounced to the beat. The solar dancers rushed to one side of the drum to escape the fume of his farts. De Cozener had just returned from his regular meditation session at the Paraday Chicken Pluck Center on Telegraph Avenue.

Round Dance described the wail of the singers as the torment of students who were not admitted to his native literature course that semester. Well, said the blonde dancer, what do the students who get in sing about? Magic, he said, and with that he invited her to an afternoon of teases and sex in his faculty office.

TOKEN WHITE

Token White was angular, slight as a spring birch, and a fierce native by adoption, not inheritance. She was born on a ranch in Wyoming, the only child of elderly parents. Nine years later her parents died in an automobile accident. The bank foreclosed on the ranch, and the court sent her to a private boarding school because she had no ancestors. There, she learned to grieve in silence and devoted her time to the practice of archery and the music of Johnny Cash.

I Still Miss Someone. . . .

The bow became a center of her eccentric nature, a means of precise meditation and survivance. She learned to hear the curve and crook of nature in the bow and to sense the wind in the arrows. Johnny Cash always touched in her a sentiment of courage.

A Boy Named Sue. . . .

Later, she became an acknowledged expert on native bows and arrows at the university and wrote a senior thesis on "The Art of Native Archery." Shortly before her conversion in the concrete she was a student research assistant at the Phoebe Apperson Hearst Museum of Anthropology. She worked on the inventories of native bones for the Native American Graves Protection and Repatriation Act. Token White did not tell the director, at the time, that she had lived and worked in the museum almost a century earlier with her friend Ishi. Naturally, her professors were astounded to learn that so bright a scholar had become an ecstatic *wiindigoo* and San Francisco Solar Dancer.

Sergeant Cloud Burst waited for her to return on the last night of her urban vision quest. Not only was she about to become the first blonde solar dancer, but she had copies of the keys to the museum ossuaries of native bones. The six other natives had started their four-night initiation in the city and had returned on time to meet the rise of father sun in the morning. Cloud Burst, a man of dares and dubious evidence, invited me to witness the grand ceremony in a bunker at Fort Cronkite near Rodeo Lagoon.

Token White started her crusade at Union Square in San Francisco. She was abandoned on a park bench with nothing more than a bow, five arrows, the simple directions to seek an urban vision on the streets, and a portable compact disc player with the hits of Johnny Cash.

Cloud Burst told her to return to the traditions of the heart and visions of the mind, celebrate the four directions, and listen to four stories on the streets but not prime numbers in hotel lobbies. Over and over she listened to the "Man in Black," "I Walk the Line," "Ring of Fire," "Understand Your Man," and "The Ballad of Ira Hayes." Then, on the fourth night in a dense fog, she walked straight to the ceremonial bunker north of the Golden Gate Bridge.

Token White drew her sacred Yahi bow a short time before dawn and launched four flaming arrows through the portals of the bunker from the four directions. The arrows bounced on the cold concrete.

Cloud Burst heard the thrum of the bowstring and said the arrows were sacred messages from the great spirit. Minutes later, another arrow landed in the bunker with a note tied over the thin shaft. Fine Print read the note to the *wiindigoo* solar dancers, and in the distance we heard the voice of Johnny Cash.

Ira Hayes. . . .

Father Cloud Burst, you trusted me to become native, and a city *wiindigoo,* and that trust lasts forever in my heart. You said you would dream about my heart, and that touched me on these four cold nights in San Francisco. No one ever said that to me, and my heart beats to your big words and the solar dance.

I write to you on brown paper tonight with a strong heart, and wait to hear my name called as a *wiindigoo* solar dancer. Johnny Cash is my vision as clear as mountain water. Ishi is my vision, and with him the vision of the bow, the natural tension of the bow. My memories are native, and my visions are with the solar dancers.

Token White waited outside the bunker to hear her name. Only then could she enter as a solar dancer. She strained to listen, and the cold wind rushed over her body, raised her blonde hair. The ocean waves seethed on the shore nearby.

Fine Print burned the note in the fire because it was tied to the fifth arrow, a prime number. The sound of the ocean wavered on the cold concrete in the bunker. Cloud Burst gestured twice in the four directions, and then raised his hands to the sun, shrouded in a haze on the horizon. He brushed his face and chest with smoke from the cedar fire and wailed in the four directions. Then he pierced the flesh on his chest with plastic skewers, over the many marbled scars of other solar dances in the bunker.

Cloud Burst leaned back to tighten the leather laces that were tied to the skewers and a pole. He danced in a wide circle around the pole at the center of the bunker and wailed to mother earth and the native *wiindigoo* cannibal monsters. The fire cracked and raised our shadows on the concrete. Injun Time danced around the pole on the other side of the bunker. Fast Food marked time in the same direction. He pounded his white feet on the concrete and left giant charcoal footprints around the fire.

Cloud Burst raised his arms, leaned back as he danced, and the taut laces hummed against his weight. Suddenly, the skewers tore holes in his thick, disfigured chest. The pole shivered, a blurred shadow on the concrete. Blood covered his great belly.

Token White, he shouted her name in the four directions, and then she was told to enter the bunker as a *wiindigoo* warrior and solar dancer. Come home with your new vision, come home to your father the sun, come home to the sacred bunker as a solar dancer.

The other solar dancers waited in silence. They were serious to a brutal fault, the mortal ruins of simulated visions in an abandoned artillery bunker. The solar dancers were ominous and never shared a moment of humor or irony. That precious tease of native trickster stories was in their absence. Johnny Cash was the only natural praise that early morning.

Token White entered the bunker with bow in hand and tears on her cheeks. She was named a native in a torturous dance, and then she was pierced with skewers and tied to the pole. She danced in circles, ecstatic to be a solar dancer at sunrise. The fog had cleared at last and bright beams of light flashed through the portals of the bunker.

Cloud Burst wrapped his arms around her from behind and pinched her small breasts. She danced in a trance, he leaned back, and the skewers tore the skin above her breasts. She shouted his name and turned in his arms. The sunrise shimmered in her blonde hair. Cloud Burst wailed and spread her warm blood on his cheeks and arms. We are here to defend mother earth and our nation, he shouted. Cloud Burst shivered with a strange sense of pain and glory.

Ring of Fire. . . .

The other solar dancers were pierced with skewers and tied to the pole. They danced in pain, but not to the bloody end. Cloud Burst and Token White were the only *wiindigoo* dancers who tore their flesh in an ecstatic vision.

ISHI OBSCURA

Token White was at boarding school, eleven years old, when she discovered natives in the book *Ishi in Two Worlds* by Theodora Kroeber. She told the solar dancers that morning how Ishi had been her very best friend until she met Cloud Burst.

Ishi, she said, taught me how to hunt with bow and arrow in the mountains near Mount Lassen. I was a survivor with him, and later we lived and worked together in the Museum of Anthropology at the University of California.

That was in the late summer, as you know, and that night we were cornered by dogs near a slaughterhouse. The sheriff took us to town and locked us in the jail. We were scared, tired, and hungry.

Ishi was alone, shouted Bad Mouth.

Ishi, you know, said Knee High.

Ishi is my story, said Token White.

Ishi was in the book, said Fine Print.

Ishi never read, said Injun Time.

Ishi hated blondes, shouted Bad Mouth.

Ishi, you know, said Knee High.

Token White insisted that she was there, in a vision, the last of his native family. Ishi was my brother, but he could not read the books we were in at the time. The sheriff showed us the local newspaper stories, that we were wild, stone agers, but news of our retreat from the mountains brought a few good white people to our cell door.

Alfred Kroeber invited us to live in the museum, and he became our best friend. Saxton Pope, the medical doctor, was an archer, and he wanted to know how to make bows and arrows. Ishi taught me how to hunt with the short bow. Pope taught me how other natives made their bows and arrows. We all learned from each other in those days.

My Yahi bow is sacred, said Token White. Ishi taught me how to make it from a single piece of mountain juniper. Listen, you can hear the deer in the sinew string, and the curve of the bow is the touch of nature. The arrows are made from hazel sticks, and we rolled them over heated stones to make them smooth. We even made points out of broken bottles.

Ishi used three feathers from a single bird wing for each arrow. The other arrows have four feathers, trimmed bird feathers, for a better spin in flight. Listen, every arrow has a particular sound, the sound of the actual bird in flight.

Saxton Pope taught me how to make other native bows, said Token White. My Mojave bow was made from a single stave of willow smoked in a cedar fire to temper the grain. The bark is still on the back of the bow. My Mojave bow, she said, is perfect on a cool morning because the wood changes with the temperature. My Yahi bow was the best one this morning.

My Navaho bow is made of mesquite wood, and this is my sweetest bow. The wood turns with a fine balance and hums with nature. My Apache bow is made from a white hickory wagon wheel hoop, the one you saw me use at the plaza the other day. Pope told me it was named a cupid bow because of the curve.

Phoebe Apperson Hearst started the museum, and her name is on the door. Ishi was always curious about her clothes. She wore a giant hat on the first day she came by to visit.

Shit, man, you were there, said Touch Tone.

Not a chance, shouted Bad Mouth.

Never, me too, said Knee High.

Benjamin Ide Wheeler came to meet us at the museum. He was the president of the University of California. Many people came by to see us in the museum. We made arrow points for some of the visitors. We were the last, you see, of the Stone Age natives, and we lived in a museum.

Fucking trickster, said Fast Food.

Token White is a chancer, said Cloud Burst.

Chancers are never, never blonde, shouted Bad Mouth. She was bored with the bow-and-arrow stories, cranky about the four-day visions, and she wanted a fast food breakfast.

Never blonde, said Knee High.

Token White turned toward the fire. Her breasts were mottled with dried blood. It hurts me now to tell you this, she said, and then spread her hands out over the cedar coals. Ishi, you know, laughed when he told his great wood duck stories, but then he started to cough blood. He was tired, and very weak, and could not even start a story. That spring he died in my arms. His blood stained my shirt and breasts, and that was on March 25, 1916.

Saxton Pope was there at our side. The doctor was a wise man, a scientist to the very end, and he cut my best friend into pieces. Ishi was cremated, part by part, but his brain was taken out, packed in a jar, and sent to some weird scientists at the Smithsonian Institution.

Ishi is my brother, my spirit vision of the past, and he is always with me in my stories. I loved him more than anyone else in the world, said Token White. Now, Cloud Burst is my *wiindigoo* father, and my great native family is complete as a solar dancer.

CANNON CLEANER

Cloud Burst was not the same man over fast food. He ate very slowly as his memories turned to the military. Cheese in a tube, hash browns, the pungent smell of bacon grease set the right mood of his service stories.

The ethnic emissaries, as you know, received many notes and scenes from other sources and sent the final narratives to me from time to time. Cloud Burst came under much closer archival scrutiny with my descriptive scenes of the solar dancers on campus that semester.

Sergeant John Martin Peterson was his name some fifty years ago in the Sixth Coastal Artillery Battery. Four traditional natives came together from the army, navy, air corps, and marines, he said over a fast food breakfast, to defend our mother earth and San Francisco from the Japanese.

Cloud Burst turned to avoid photographers and he never answered questions, not even simple queries about directions. He was dark and morose over the drum, ecstatic on the skewers, a *wiindigoo* at night on the campus, and plainly nostalgic over fast food in the morning. The bunker was the center of his military service and solar dance stories.

My first vision was in the bunker, he told the native ruck of solar dancers. Natives who write stories have no real visions, he said, and then ordered more pancakes. You see, written stories have no sound or silence. The curse was not directed at me, but the solar dancers stared at me anyway.

Cloud Burst once tried to write stories, but he could not create more than the obvious. By word he was literal, evasive, nostalgic, and teased no sense of irony. He was a solar dancer, a gloomy man of mundane silence with the wounds of an eerie *wiindigoo* vision.

Cloud Burst never mentioned any native relatives, family, community, or more of an actual past than his military bunker service. Sergeant John Martin Peterson, according to a narrative from the ethnic emissaries, enlisted in the United States Army to avoid criminal prosecution on the White Earth Reservation in Minnesota. There was no evidence, however, that he was native. Nothing more than a trace of an unmarried ancestor in a photograph. The medical narrative indicated that he had been demoted twice for subversive activities, namely, the practice of shamanism, black magic, tricky malingering, and primitive ceremonies.

Sergeant Cloud Burst was stationed at Fort Cronkhite, across the Golden Gate Bridge from San Francisco. He was ordered to test fire the first sixteen-inch casemated cannons out to sea, he said, and the concrete bunkers resisted the shock of the big guns. He served in the harbor defense unit, until the end of the war.

The ethnic emissaries noted in the medical narrative that his first ecstatic vision took place on Wednesday, 1 April 1942, during the full moon of the fourth month, four hours before dawn at the coastal defense bunker overlooking Rodeo Lagoon near San Francisco, California. Saturn, Mars, and Jupiter were the evening stars.

The sergeant vanished on that date, and he was gone for four nights. The narrative indicated that he was wounded, amnesiac, and hospitalized on his return. His fingernails were black and his face was burned in a vision, he said, a vision of solar dancers. Later, he told a doctor that he was alone in the bunker at the time of his vision. He saw a solar fire burst out of the ocean and soar over the bunker. He said a black rain burned his face.

I was carried into space on a magic star, he told a military psychiatrist. The mongrels took me for a wild ride in a cloud-burst, and so that became my nickname. Sirius, the Dog Star, was bright in the constellation Canis Major.

The sergeant vanished twice more in a vision, and the last time he became a *wiindigoo* in magical flight, a solar dancer over the coastal bunker. He was demoted without a court martial and served as a cannon cleaner for the duration of the war.

Cloud Burst became a heinous mediator of wicked visions and sensations, but not an ecstatic shaman or native healer. His visions were satanic, and the tricksters of shame must have burned his face for the lies that night in the bunker. Since then his stories have been burdened with separation, violence, and victimry.

Shamans bear the memories of nature, escape distances, the ecstasies of resurrection, and a native presence. Shamans overturn time in a dangerous rush of contrary visions and tricky stories that tease a native sense of absence. Forever, the *wiindigoo* monsters are treasonous, the vicious tithers of native visions and ironic, succored victimry. The solar dancers are *wiindigoo,* the mutant vampires of the concrete and the war with the Japanese.

Shamans tease the native chancers with ecstatic visions and stories. The cures of absence are stories, the tricky traces of a native presence, and by turns a continuous creation. The ecstatic solar dancers were never storiers of presence. They were the apostles of an ironic absence, and they resurrected native chancers by sinister curses, resentment, possession, sacrifice, and victimry.

WETLAND SOVEREIGNTY

Come to our reservation
on refuse mountain
to meditate on waste,
and rise above
the word wars,
wild stench,
peace names,
plastic pictures,
and terminal creeds.
Come meditate on my
Waste Mountain Reservation.

PONTIUS BOOKER

Provost Pontius Booker was on his way to a customary lunch meeting with his colleagues at the Faculty Club. The air was clean after an overnight storm, and the trees were bright. The provost must have paused, as usual, to admire the bay laurel in the arbor, and then he crossed the narrow bridge over Strawberry Creek.

The police announced that the provost had vanished on his usual course somewhere between the bridge and the foyer of the Faculty Club. His body was never found, but several weeks later the campus glazier discovered blood stains and giant footprints in Senior Hall. Only one person reported seeing a strange creature about that time near the creek. The police portrait of a sinister man, as you know, turned out to be a retired historian and her wolfhound.

Fine Print had marked the provost earlier with that blue scapegoat character of death, the sign of the *wiindigoo* monster on his shoulder. Then, two weeks later, he crossed the same bridge, and the entire sinister ruck of solar dancers was there for the abduction of the provost. He was, as you know, the very first solar sacrifice of atonement for the millions of native chancers.

Token White, later that summer, told me the bloody, gruesome stories of the many abductions and *wiindigoo* sacrifices. She could have been a naive character in a trickster scene, or so it seemed to me at the time, but she was obsessed, not ironic, when she told me the explicit stories of the actual sacrifices. The provost and the other abusers were beheaded and fleshed. Later, their brains were removed and preserved in a bucket, and their heads, as you know, begot the resurrection of the native chancers.

Folsom Prison Blues. . . .

Bad Mouth touched the provost as he paused in the arbor. She sneered and hissed at him, an omen of the cold *wiindigoo* monster, and then, as he turned to cross the bridge, she moaned, moved close to his side, and warned him that she had a pistol in her pocket. The provost must have thought she was a paranoid druggie, or a discontented student angry about a final letter grade. Surely, he assured her not to worry as they walked along the path near the creek. The provost, of course, could have easily changed a grade to save his life, but he had no idea that he was about to be sacrificed by solar dancers in a log cabin behind the Faculty Club.

The solar dancers were posted around the cabin, ready to distract anyone who might cross their wicked paths in the red-woods. The area was shrouded by the giant trees, and few people used the paths. Cloud Burst parked his minivan nearby in the loading zone at the rear of the Faculty Club.

Bad Mouth pushed the provost through the side door of Senior Hall. The Order of the Golden Bear, a secret society of senior men, was founded there more than a century ago. The namesake cabin was once the rustic heart of the campus, but the massive log building had been abandoned for more than thirty years.

Pontius Booker was blindfolded with a red bandanna, and his hands were tied behind his back. The cabin was dark, iso-lated, and he would never survive, so why the blindfold? Token White told me that she shunned the mortal gaze of those sacrificed. She learned as a hunter to avoid the wild, pathetic eyes of an animal close to death, but, at the last minute, she removed the blindfold on the provost and covered her own eyes. She was, after all, a meditative archer.

That terrible ruck of solar dancers cursed and tormented the provost, their first sacrifice for the native chancers. They cut and tore at his sports coat in a rage, and then removed his necktie, shirt, and trousers. The dancers cursed the color of his skin, his pompous manner, and they even mentioned how he had insulted me and my sacred name two weeks earlier. The stories bothered me, of course, that he should remember my

name in the last tormented moments of his life. Token White
assured me, however, that the abuse turned bloody and the
provost had more to think about than my name. I did not
overreact, because she might not have told me the details of
the other sacrifices and the resurrection of native chancers.

Knee High, she said, stole his money and wore the provost's
golden bear necktie around his waist like a trophy. Later, the
solar dancers removed and destroyed credit cards, spectacles,
rings, keys, every object of identity. Beheaded, only a pale
memory of the provost could be traced to the resurrection of
native chancers.

The solar dancers painted the character of the dead on his
bare chest, the ominous mark of *wiindigoo* sacrifice and atonement for the native chancers. Token White said the provost
worried more about the appearance of his nude body than
about his imminent death.

The solar dancers taunted the naked, pursy provost. His
chest was narrow, but he had a great potbelly. Injun Time
spread a sheet of black plastic on the floor in front of the fireplace and then pushed the provost into the center. Token White
said he should have known, then and there, what was about
to happen, but instead he showed more embarrassment than
fear. He tried to hide his tiny penis by leaning forward, but the
solar dancers pulled his legs apart and poked at his testicles.

Knee High threw things at the provost, a fast food carton,
an aluminum can, a tape dispenser, wastebasket, fireplace
wood, but he was restrained by the other solar dancers when
he raised a wooden bench over his head. Actually, the logs of
the cabin were so thick that no one outside could hear a sound.

Token White said the provost never fought back or tried to escape. She hated his pompous manner on the campus, but she was touched by his sense of modesty. Pontius, she said, had such a tiny penis that he lost his fear of death.

Senior Hall was divided by a massive fireplace. The main section was on one side, and on the other, the once secret chambers of the senior men. The provost was tormented in the secret room at first and then sacrificed at the fireplace in the main hall.

My Mojave bow waited to be touched that afternoon, said Token White. The cabin remained cool in the shadows of the giant redwoods, and the provost shivered right down to his sallow toenails. The temperature was just right to use her tempered willow bow. The solar dancers teased and taunted the provost, a lonesome, wretched man slouching naked on a sheet of black plastic. Sadly, he was no more than thirty feet, at the time of his death, from the academic manners of his colleagues in the Faculty Club.

Token White raised her bow, an ancient motion. She must have turned to the window, to the wisps of thin, natural light, and steadied her breath, a meditative pose. Slowly, she reached above her head. I have seen her do this many times, the meditation, not the actual sacrifice. Then she braced the bow, never distracted by the ordinary presence of others. Truly, she becomes the natural tension of the string, the bow, and the rush of the arrow, a precise moment of meditation, native transmotion, and absolute peace.

Token White transcended the technical mastery of native archery only after she had practiced for more than twenty years. She told me that the moment came not by the sound of the string, or by the great flight of the arrow, or even, as a child, by her mastery of the slingshot, but by her experiences with chickens. Yes, curiously, she discovered transcendence in the natural reason of an escape distance. Chickens, animals, and other birds transcend their fear of humans and death at an aesthetic escape distance. There is no expectation, she said, no manners or dominance. The chicken has the common sense of a natural escape distance.

She could never bear to study archery with anyone, as you might have expected, because she always knew more than her teachers. I once told her about *Zen in the Art of Archery* by Eugen Herrigel, but she raised her bow and teased me that words lack the natural grace of bows and arrows. She meant, of course, the arrows she learned how to make with Ishi in Northern California.

Token White raised her bow, nocked an arrow on the string, and waited at the end of the cabin. The *wiindigoo* solar dancers must have been aroused by the aesthetic and meditative moment of sacrifice. They turned in silence and moved to the side, out of range. The provost must have sensed that his escape distance was about to end that afternoon.

She was an archer of transcendence, and, at the same time, she was an ecstatic solar dancer. That contradiction has never been an easy story. Suddenly, in a state of concentration and meditation, the primacy of a natural transcendence, she turned to resentment and sacrifice. Only at the commencement would she restore a balance, a final native atonement, but those scenes, as you know, come much later in the narrative.

The *wiindigoo* monster lures those who have been weak-
ened by contradictions, and devours the insecure with authentic stories. The monster comes out of the cold winter wind,
and waits in the haze on the thresholds of common deceit and
shame. Cloud Burst and the solar dancers were lured by the
wiindigoo monster to a feral escape distance in the city.

Token White, the shaman archer, becomes the bow, the arrow,
and the target by meditation, not by remorse, shame, or victimry.
She pierced her breasts to become a solar dancer, and she has
never been insecure since that bloody ceremony in the bunker.

Ishi was her native vision, as you know, and then the morose
Cloud Burst became her solar dance father. So, you can see
why natives need trickster stories to distract the monster of
sacrifice and authenticity.

The *wiindigoo* monster is not a tradition, but a wicked, cultural separation, and the customary sacrifice is the other side
of victimry. The arrow of the shaman pierces two hearts, one
aesthetic, straight to the cold heart of cultural dominance, and
the other a natural scapegoat. The solar dancers are demonic,
touched by the monster, and authentic only by separation and
sacrifice, but not aesthetic, ironic, or tricky. The solar dancers
are the best reason for trickster stories, to liberate the mind
from a hazy winter and nasty separations.

Token White raised her bow and as a shaman aimed the
arrow at her own heart. Her transcendence was an aesthetic
motion, a sense of death and, at the same time, a native survivance. She soon overcame the contradictions of violence and
aesthetic archery, the naive other at the very heart of sacrifice
and atonement. She aimed at her own heart to sacrifice the

other, she told me, to resurrect the native chancers, and by that she meant survivance.

Token White wore a blue mask and told the solar dancers to remove the blindfold on the provost. She sensed his presence, and shunned the scared animal in his eyes. Cloud Burst prepared the scene of the sacrifice. He cut the provost four times, thin bloody lines across his chest, and then untied his hands. The provost moaned, and touched his wounds. Blood covered his potbelly.

Token White turned in a circle, as in a dance, steadied her breath at an escape distance, and then she released the arrow with a narrow obsidian point. The sound of the bowstring, the wind of the arrow, and the rush of breath were connected in an instance of sacrifice. The arrow pierced the heart of the provost. He turned, reached for the feathers on the arrow, and then doubled over in front of the fireplace. Slowly, he lost his breath.

Bad Mouth decapitated and dissected the provost. His head was stored in a plastic bucket. Later, his brain was removed, as you know, and his treated skull would liberate a native chancer in the museum.

Cloud Burst and the other solar dancers bound the butchered remains of the provost in black plastic. The bloody chunks of flesh and bone were later thrown to the mountain lions and coyotes on a remote trail in the Charles Lee Tilden Regional Park.

PENIS ENVY

Four Skins sat at the kitchen table with three tiny terriers, and at night he shared the big bed with his puppeteer. He was the master puppet of the house, always at his best, and he slept in the nude. The terriers, ever wary of his presence, crouched at the bottom of the bed.

Ruby Blue Welcome lives on top of the mountain, or so she says several times a day. She works that mountain into her lectures and stories, but she told me once that she would rather live alone on an island surrounded by the eternal sound of waves. Actually, she boasts of solitude in her stories only to overcome a desperate sense of social separation.

Albany Hill was her mountain, and her narrow townhouse was connected to seventeen others, each one with a postcard view of San Francisco Bay. There, at the end of the academic day, alone with her loyal puppet and tiny terriers, she watched western movies on television. Nightly, at the end of the movies, a massive fog rushed through the Golden Gate.

Four Skins is my man, she boasted.

Bad Mouth resented more people than she could ever name, but she was obsessed with that hand puppet. She was determined to dismember the awkward cloth body and pickle his hollow plastic head with the brains of the others that were sacrificed that semester. She tried many times to abduct the puppet, but each time she failed to get past the burglar alarm system.

Knee High, her tetchy brother, carried out her obsessions by name and notion, as you know, and he climbed through a narrow bathroom window one foggy night, slithered across the bedroom floor, and snatched the puppet right out of the arms of his mistress. The terriers were silent, complicit in the abduction of the privileged puppet. Naturally, the abduction became a series of stories about the geek of the mountain, enhanced by a crude plastic coitus interruptus, and every version of the story brought tears of vengeance to the eyes of the solar dancers. No other sacrifice was told so many times and with such great pleasure.

Token White shot the puppet twice. Once with her slingshot as the puppet sat with the solar dancers at a picnic bench, and then with her bow. The stone dented his plastic forehead.

Four Skins was tied to a cedar tree near the creek at Live Oak Park in Berkeley. Knee High poked the puppet with a stick, his rude measure of sacrifice. Fast Food burned his plastic nose with a black cigar. Token White nocked a stout arrow with a flaked green glass point and shot the puppet straight through his canvas heart. Four Skins was draped over an arrow lodged in the cedar. Cloud Burst beat a morbid strain on the wooden bench and his wicked ruck danced around the puppet. Several park sleepers joined them in the dance.

Bad Mouth severed his head and sealed it into a Mason jar. She jerked at his enormous penis, and then hacked it loose with a jackknife. Knee High ripped out a plastic hand and cracked it open like a bone between his teeth. Fine Print tore a leg out, and each solar dancer removed at least one part of the puppet. The plastic parts were crushed and cremated on a barbecue grill at the park. Only his penis was spared.

Four Skins was put on sale, a partial repatriation, a few days later at the Phoebe Apperson Hearst Museum of Anthropology. Injun Time and the other solar dancers distracted the sales clerk in the museum shop during the actual commercial repatriation of the puppet. Bad Mouth placed his brown penis upright in a display case with figures of saints, amulets, and miracle charms. The penis was decorated with a beaded head-band and two tiny bells. Knee High spread the ashes of the puppet in the anthropology library.

The museum director discovered the penis a few days later, after several visitors had complained, and reasoned that it was another anthropology dildo joke. She covered the penis with paper towels and threw it in the trash. Later, a street person rescued the puppet penis on his regular rounds of the dumpsters and sold it to a student on Telegraph Avenue. The student wore the penis as an amulet on campus.

Four Skins, that was my penis, shouted Blue Welcome. She had recognized the distinctive organ one morning and told the student that it was part of her missing puppet. The student was amused, of course, that a faculty member would lay claim to a dildo, but she would not part with her penile amulet for love or money.

EROTIC OSTEOLOGY

Doctor Paul Snow, the senior museum osteologist, was aroused by native skeletons. Truly, the absence of natives, the actual skeletal remains of our ancestors, became his most erotic sense of academic presence. Daily, the fantasies of flesh and muscle excited him as he touched cranium, pelvis, femur, radius, ribs, and other bones. Several crania and pelves were mounted on his laboratory bench in the most suggestive positions.

Snow Boy, an excavation nickname, fingered the smooth orbital eye bones of the crania in moments of scholarly rumination. Nothing was more erotic to him than the thought of unrestrained sex with a primitive native woman in a circle of crania. Many of the native skulls that he selected on his bench were stolen, traded, and then caged forever in the museum. Snow Boy had probably fancied sex with every cranium in the collection.

This famous anthropologist and osteologist was virtually raised on human bones. His unmarried mother was a graduate student in archaeology, and, worried that she would be denied a research grant, disguised her pregnancy. Snow Boy was born in silence at a remote excavation in Ethiopia.

Snow Boy was an awkward hominid, a site child who created mutant, osseous creatures out of bones, and then, as an adolescent, he envisioned their carnal parts. He masturbated more than once over the remains of native coastal women. The bones were stolen by his mother and held in osteological bondage.

Snow Boy was short, his cheeks and calves were thick, and he was always disheveled and untidy. His hair was long, tangled, and mostly gray. He carried bones around in his pockets, and always lectured with a bone in hand. Many times he tried to write on the blackboard with a bone. Native bones were his aphrodisiac, but his wife never shared his peculiar passions for human remains. He once told a curator at the museum that his wife banned bones in his own house. Bones are out, his wife announced after the birth of their second child. She ruled that his bones remain in the museum at the university. So, his obsession with bones became more than a mere learned practice. Naturally, when an actual, mature, fleshy native woman entered his empire of bones, his fate was sealed on the very first night.

Ruby Blue Welcome told me that she was the source of his erotic pleasure, but she seemed rather desperate to boast of his sexual obsessions. Someone would mention his name and that started her wild sex stories. She became the actual flesh and bones of his wanton, erotic osteology.

I know this sounds incredible, and satirical, but remember that she was the most literal person in native studies and rather short on a sense of irony. Trickster stories were never considered in her rare moments of creation and memory. That she boasted about a sex adventure with a singular bone man was ironic enough, but later her stories were confirmed by several curators and research assistants in the museum.

So, was he aroused by certain bones?

Naturally, said Blue Welcome.

Show me, show me, which ones?

Skulls, he fingers eye sockets.

Eye sockets, what did he do to them?

Don't get personal, said Blue Welcome.

The bones were a distraction, she said, the first few times they had sex, but then she was actually excited by the idea that some of her native ancestors might have been right there on the bench as bone voyeurs.

They had panic sex several times a month on his laboratory bench in the museum. The best time, of course, was late at night, but they also had sex over lunch. The native bones were stored on trays, locked in cages, in an underground area of the museum. The bone vault was secured by motion detectors and several locked doors.

Snow Boy was certain that no one could ever surprise them in the act. Once, however, their own heated motion activated the alarms. Their orgasms were wild, she said, a tribute to the bones and crania. Blue Welcome was convinced that the bone sex actually stimulated her research on the Ghost Dance Religion.

Token White worked as a research assistant in the museum and heard stories about their encounters on the bone bench. She was too embarrassed by sex, even the mere mention of the act, to consider the stories that she had heard about the wild bone man and his native woman.

Native bones were sacred in her restrained order of nature, and she worked on the museum inventories only to name and rebury native bones under the Native American Graves Protection and Repatriation Act.

She was aroused and shamed late one night as she reviewed the museum records of the haunted native crania that had been stolen by grave robbers, sold to bone traders, and then, she said, sold again at the turn of the century to the restaurateur and hotelier Ford Ferguson Harvey.

Token White touched and consoled each stolen cranium. She prayed over each bone tray in the cage. That discovery and the sounds she heard that night in the museum were critical moments in her conversion to the violence of the *wiindigoo* solar dancers.

The sound carried over the top of the many cages of human remains. She was working in one of the crania cages at the very back of the museum and heard whispers, then familiar voices in the distance. At first she was only distracted by the sound of teasing and laughter in so sacred a place. She treated native bones as if they were rare manuscripts in a monastic library. She was curious, however, about the sound of furniture being moved in the caged osteology laboratory. Finally, she was overwrought by the sound of animal moans and erotic grunts.

Blue Welcome never wore underclothes when she visited her bone lover in the museum. They had agreed to have sudden, panic sex with their clothes on. Just in case someone entered the museum, they would have time to appear academic. They had sex only in the museum because he was insecure and impotent in any other place. She tried to seduce him several times in her townhouse, but he had no erotic sense outside of the museum, no lust without his circle of bones, and he was suspicious of the puppet. Four Skins stared at him, and the terriers snapped at his calves.

Snow Boy wore pleated, baggy trousers and boxer shorts. He was untidy and always prepared for sudden, upright sex among the bones. Blue Welcome wore a thin cotton summer dress on the night that they were seen in the museum by Token White.

I was on my way to the encryption center that same night and encountered the lusty puppeteer on the plaza. I understood later why she seemed to be out of breath. No doubt the mere thought of sex with the bone man on his laboratory bench aroused her for hours ahead of time. She was otherwise an isolated, lonesome person, and only the nasty solar dancers would fault her peculiar pleasures in a circle of native bones. We talked for a few minutes, but she was elusive, and she marked time in the direction of the museum.

Four Skins out for the night?

No, he's at home, said Blue Welcome.

Preparing his lecture?

Don't be stupid.

Nice night for a walk.

Yes, said Blue Welcome.

Her skin was moist, and her lips parted slightly with each short breath, almost a sensual pant. The coarse cotton draped over her huge nipples, and as she turned and hurried to the museum the white cotton rode high on her thighs. Only later was her mission revealed in several stories.

Token White moved closer to the sounds of sex that night and crouched behind a cabinet of femurs and pelves. From there, outside the osteology cage, only a few feet from the laboratory bench, she could see them between the shelves of bones.

Blue Welcome leaned back against the bench, raised her dress slightly, and spread her legs. She touched her inner thighs and moaned. The cotton had absorbed the sweat on her crotch and belly. Snow Boy moved closer, his every breath a primal grunt. I imagine she unzipped his fly and reached into his trousers. Naturally, he unbuttoned the top of her cotton dress and touched her breasts. She heaved and he thrust to the sensation of her hand on his stout penis. They pawed each other and then he raised her dress and pushed his hand into her crotch. She shouted and then moaned louder, a wild sound that echoed in the museum.

Snow Boy leaned forward and she touched his testicles with one hand and stroked his penis with the other. He bounced on his toes, an animal dance, and turned from side to side.

Then he raised her buttocks onto the bench, spread her legs, and brushed her wet crotch with his stout penis. She watched his moves and fingered his testicles. Suddenly, he thrust his penis into her cunt and then they both leaned into the circle of crania on the bench. She wrapped her legs around his thighs. He sucked her breasts and, at the same time, he must have touched one of seven crania on the back of the bench. He thrust, once, twice, and leaned back to see her cunt, then pushed again more firmly. Deeply, he held onto her hips with both hands and moved in a wide circle. She grabbed the back of his shirt and pulled him closer, even tighter, pumping her thighs in a wild motion. Token White told me the bench moved, the crania bounced, and one hit the cement floor.

Blue Welcome turned, trembled, and cried out in the voice of panic cox. Snow Boy pushed harder, shivered, grunted, and then ejaculated. They clutched each other on the bench, and the sound of their primal breath echoed in every cranium and caged bone in the museum.

Token White caught her breath as she crouched behind a tray of bones. She watched the last thrust and heard the last moan that night. She was aroused, sickened, and disconcerted by the scene, and, at the same time, she resented their brazen abuse of native remains. That night was the start of her conversion. She would become a solar dancer and liberate the native chancers.

Blue Welcome cleaned her crotch and twittered over the crania on the bench. Snow Boy had already turned to his research, the dimensions of orbital bones in coastal native cultures. She pushed her toes into the skull that had bounced to the floor, raised it above her head, and then pitched it in the air.

Token White watched in horror as the skull landed on the bench and rolled into the others. She caught her breath a second time, but not for the same reason. Blue Welcome, she told me much later, was a decadent native and deserved to die for her abuse of sacred bones, but at the time she gave me no indication that she was the one who carried out the actual sacrifice of the bone lovers right there in the museum. Later, she told me the double sacrifice story.

PORTENTOUS CONNECTION

Cloud Burst was a master of resentment, as you know, and he was driven by a gruesome *wiindigoo* vision to resurrect by sacrifice the remains of native chancers. That frightful vision of the solar dancers was undeniable, but the actual access to the bones needed more than enmity and ecstasy. The actual portentous connection was ironic, a blonde student research assistant who would fight with the devil to protect natives and their bones. Now, at last, the actual keys to carry out his vision were close at hand. Token White provided the electronic codes and keys to what would become the museum of native chancers.

Several weeks after the *wiindigoo* ceremonies in the bunker and the sacrifice of the provost in the redwood cabin, the solar dancers carried out a spectacular double sacrifice. The location of the gruesome crime, of course, was the Phoebe Apperson Hearst Museum of Anthropology.

Blue Welcome mourned over the absence of her beloved Four Skins. She tried many times to persuade the student to return the penis, but the student teased the association of the amulet. Finally, she demanded money. Blue Welcome, however, refused to pay the cruel and inhuman ransom for any part of Four Skins. She was convinced that her puppet had been abducted by the solar dancers, but she said nothing in public, and so denied them the pleasure of her pain. Only a week before her death she hired a former student to recover the penis, but he was arrested in the act and the penile amulet was seized by the university police as evidence.

Snow Boy became her bone man, but she told me, after the students teased her, that he was no substitute for Four Skins. She was dependent on the love of her puppet, but everything in her life changed when he was gone. Her tiny terriers, for instance, took over the bed, and she dressed more often for those wild nights of panic sex on the bone bench in the museum. The most exciting moments of her life were with bones, not with her terriers.

Token White could not bear to work in the museum after the faculty had defiled and abused native bones. The director granted her a leave, not knowing the real reason, so that she could complete her senior thesis on "The Art of Native Archery." Only the solar dancers knew at the time that the cruel sacrifice of the bone-bench lovers would be the resurrection of native chancers.

Blue Welcome was the faculty representative at a reception for new students and their parents a few hours before she died in the arms of her bone man. She told the students and parents about the early days of native studies on the campus. Actually, she told rather tricky stories for a change only to disguise her emotions over the absence of Four Skins. She always brought the puppet along to receptions and other ceremonies, dressed in his tiny black robe and bright, feathered headdress, and together they entertained the students. Many parents wrote letters to the chancellor about the marvelous, erotic dances of the puppet, truly a colorful native tradition. The more conservative parents, however, worried about the academic future of native studies.

Blue Welcome wore a pleated linen skirt and sleeveless blouse under her black academic robe. Following the reception and polite conversation over finger food she went directly to her bone man for panic sex on the bone bench. That was the night of their terminal orgasms in the museum.

Cloud Burst and the solar dancers used the electronic codes and duplicate keys to enter the museum during the reception for new students. They decorated their faces with the calligraphy of death, the very same blue characters that marked the provost and the puppet, and waited in the cage near the bone bench for the erotic moment of *wiindigoo* sacrifice.

Snow Boy was at a conference seminar on osteology and arrived late with his leather briefcase full of bones. He removed two crania, sorted other bone bits and pieces into several trays, and then turned to finger the crania on the bench. The orbital bones were burnished by his constant touch and finger motion. Only when he heard his native bone lover at the door did he see the crude blue character on his briefcase.

Blue Welcome knocked four times, paused, and then twice more on the metal door. The sound thundered in the long tunnel to the bone cages. She must have marked time at the door, as she did once when we met on the plaza. She was aroused by the mere thought and secrecy of sex in the bone museum.

Token White told me that Blue Welcome, once inside, caught the bone man by the crotch and towed him to the bone bench. Blue Welcome leaned back, raised her robe, spread her moist thighs, and moaned for panic sex. Snow Boy, however, was distracted by the mark on her academic hood.

What's that?

My hood, said Blue Welcome.

No, the blue mark, said Snow Boy.

Nothing, nothing.

That same mark is on my briefcase.

Never mind, said Blue Welcome.

Blue Welcome reached for his penis and with both hands pulled him closer, but he resisted her touch for the first time since he shared her bed with the puppet. He slowly backed out of her legs, raised his head, and stared into the shadows of the bone cages. He must have sensed there was someone in the museum.

Token White ducked to avoid his wild eyes, but later he turned with an arrow in his heart and she was caught and shamed forever in his last mortal gaze. Cloud Burst was not worried about being seen because the bone abusers would die sooner or later that same night. The solar dancers had planned to sacrifice them at the very climax of panic sex.

Blue Welcome was steadfast about sex with her bone man, not aware at the time that her orgasm would be terminal. She

unzipped her robe, raised her blouse, shouted his name, and
the pitch of her voice bounced on the concrete. Then she leaned
back on the bench, reached above her head, seized two skulls,
and mounted them over her bare breasts.

Snow Boy thrust his fingers through the orbital bones and
touched her nipples at the same time. She jerked his penis until
it was hard again. He butted her thighs, stroked her crotch,
and then pushed his penis deep into her cunt. Naturally, the
wild hominid snorted several times to punctuate his erotic
moves. She clenched his body between her legs and heaved
her thighs at the same time. She trembled, his buttocks quivered, and the skulls bounced on her breasts and the bone
bench.

Blue Welcome shouted and shivered with her bone man.
The solar dancers were aroused by the lust and fury of the
scene on the bench, but they waited for the precise erotic
moment of sacrifice. Bad Mouth pinched her crotch and wagged
her thighs behind the cage. Knee High masturbated with one
hand in his pocket. Injun Time folded his hands together and
sucked his thumbs. Fast Food licked the back of his hands.
Touch Tone fingered her hard black nipples. The solar dancers
were vicious voyeurs of panic sex on the bone bench.

Token White said the solar dancers almost forgot why they
were in the museum. Cloud Burst raised his head in another
trance, and then reached for Token White. He clutched her
breasts with one hand and unbuttoned his trousers with the
other. She was aroused by the sight of his giant penis, and told
me that it was much larger than she had imagined at the solar
dances. He ejaculated the instant she touched his testicles. The

thick white globs ran down her arm. She wiped it on his shirt and readied her bow for the sacrifice.

Snow Boy shivered and then paused only to be overcome by an orgasm. Blue Welcome heaved her thighs, clutched his shirt, and then held back the very last moment of panic sex. They both shouted, shuddered, and collapsed on the bone bench.

Token White raised her Apache bow, the cupid bow that she made from a hickory wagon wheel hoop. She nocked an arrow with a wide obsidian point, a long, burnished arrow with white feathers, and waited in the forsaken shadows of the museum.

Cloud Burst and the solar dancers circled the sweaty lovers on the bone bench. Bad Mouth cursed them, and the sound of her nasty voice at the end of an orgasm must have been the last worst moment of their lives. The shimmers of their panic sex were exposed to the horror of the solar dancers and their curses. That was a cruel moment of atonement.

Snow Boy turned his head to see who had violated his empire of the bones. He moved back and, at the same time, reached to cover his penis. The arrow struck his back at a slight angle and tore right down to the base of the white feathers. The rush of air and muted crush of flesh and bone was an eerie sound in the museum. Token White moved closer to the scene of the double sacrifice. She reached for the white feathers on the arrow and was caught forever in the last, panic gaze of Snow Boy.

Blue Welcome and her bone man were sacrificed by the same arrow of atonement. The obsidian point cut clear through both of their hearts. Snow Boy moaned and then died in the arms and legs of his native lover. The arrow held them together for several minutes on the bone bench. Blue Welcome died as she whispered the name of her puppet, Four Skins.

Dead Four Skins, shouted Bad Mouth.

Snow Boy too, mocked Knee High.

Token White ducked the dead gaze of the bone man as she cut the end of the arrow to save the white feathers. Snow Boy wheezed, and the last thin breath murmured in the bloody hole as she moved the arrow in his chest and heart.

Cloud Burst spread several sheets of thick black plastic under the bone bench to catch the blood. Knee High painted a giant blue *wiindigoo* character on the bone bench. Fast Food lighted a black cigar and nosed around the bone museum with the other solar dancers.

This is our stuff, said Injun Time.

My head could be here, said Fast Food.

Not a chance, said Touch Tone.

Fast Food stole a trade axe on the way out of the museum and pretended to menace the solar dancers. The university police once more reported blood stains and giant footprints, as you know, on the floor of the museum.

Bad Mouth and her brother dissected the bodies in a morbid frenzy. The heads were stored in a bucket, and the bloody body parts were bound in plastic. Later that night the solar dancers tossed the bloody parts to the mountain lions that had feasted on the provost in the park. Months later a few bones were found, but forensic tests indicated someone other than the *wiindigoo* sacrifices.

AZHETAA CENTER

Sober Browne convinced the wicked solar dancers that he was a survivance shaman, and in a whisper he boasted the resurrection of more than seven hundred native chancers. Many of those chancers were older students. His elusive, shamanic ecstasies were persuasive, but the natives he named in the elaborate ceremonies were unaware of their own resurrections.

Sobrius Mormorando, Johnny Cash, Winnie Graves, Leslie Silko, Trigger New Taste, Louis Owens, Almost Browne, Thomas King, Mighty Joe Myers, Window Peters, Gordon Light People, Elizabeth Cooker, Manly Momaday, Ward Churchill, Chicago Two Rivers, Roberta Eel, Pepa Chiricahua, Clementina Vezina, Karaoke Karkavelas, The Tabernacle Choir, and hundreds of others were counted as native chancers in his sober resurrection ceremonies.

Seven is a wicked number, shouted Bad Mouth.

Bad number, mocked Knee High.

Eight hundred natives, whispered Sober.

Good choice, said Touch Tone.

Sober was born at home on the reservation. Mouthy, his lonesome mother, told me that her only son was born with a stutter because she was teased by a native trickster, and then that same trickster healed the hesitant boy with sweet brandy. Truly, the boy never stuttered a word when he was high on liquor.

Mouthy Browne was heartsick that her son would not attend school without a drink. He was scared that he might stutter, so she left the reservation to find a cure in California.

First she contacted a distant relative who owned his very own reservation. Come and see me, he once told her, when you're down and out and ready to meditate on your own refuse. Mouthy was serious and thought he meant more than trash, rather a chance to spurn the obvious. Many natives would have moved in a cultural minute, but it was hard to believe that a native could own a sovereign reservation in the city.

Mouthy and Sober are distant cousins of Almost, China, Tune, Slyboots, Eternal Flame, Father Mother, Tulip, and Conk Browne of Bad Medicine Lake and Patronia on the White Earth Reservation in Minnesota. An eccentric crossblood family. Almost, for instance, started the first dog driver school on the reservation and placed hundreds of mongrels as chauffeurs and rural school bus drivers.

Martin Bear Charme was a natural scavenger, a survivance shaman who created a refuse reservation on San Francisco Bay. He was removed by the federal government to the city to study welding, but the war was over and he was bored with scrap metal connections, so he turned his attention to the obvious, trash collection, and made a million dollar mountain out of waste. The Bureau of Indian Affairs recognized his native claim of wetland sovereignty as the Waste Mountain Reservation.

Come to our place in the waste to meditate, chanted Bear Charme. Come to our reservation on refuse mountain to meditate on waste, and rise above the word wars, wild stench, peace names, plastic pictures, and terminal creeds. Come meditate on my Waste Mountain Reservation.

Mouthy and her tipsy son arrived at the Waste Mountain Reservation late one afternoon in the summer and were saluted by hundreds of noisy gulls. The giant sun teased the ripe waste on the mountain and then shimmered in wide, glorious banners over San Francisco Bay.

Bear Charme made millions of dollars on waste, and then, high on sovereignty, he decided to return something to the community that had made his fortune possible. Overnight he founded a refuse meditation center on his mountain. Truly, we are the garbage, the master wasters, he told his disciples. There is no way to separate ourselves, neat and clean, from the trash we dump out back, because we are the waste. Remember, we are the out and the back, and we cannot refuse our own refuse.

Bear Charme was marvelous, she told me, but the stench of garbage made her sick and the meditation sessions on solid waste bored her to tears, even with a generous scholarship. Sober could not meditate because he stuttered, and so he drank to be at peace on refuse mountain. Mouthy finally had the courage to leave the mountain when the great meditator announced that he was about to break ground to build the Refuse Casino on Waste Mountain Reservation.

Old Darkhorse, that wise survivance shaman and founder of the Half Moon Bay Skin Dip, came to the rescue in the nick of time. First he darkened her light skin so that she could find work in native services, and then he cured her son with an undertone. Mouthy was darker and much more confident, but she never left Half Moon Bay. She moved in with the old man, and to this day she works as a color consultant at the celebrated Skin Dip.

Old Darkhorse observed that the boy would not stutter when he was drunk or when he whispered. So, the color shaman gave him a new nickname. Sober attended a private school and worked with his mother at the Skin Dip. He learned how to tease the skin color secrets out of native healers, teachers, museum directors, cutthroats, firebrands, the solar dancers, and other beasts of cultural prey. By chance his undertone was an inspiration to others, and he convinced many natives that a turn in the color of their skin was no less than resurrection. Several years later he created by whispers a center of meditative rumors, native secrets, and resurrections. His undertone stories cured stutterers, alcoholics, the wicked hints of separation and victimry. Many natives have been toned and resurrected by the hush and murmur of his tricky backward stories.

The Azhetaa Center for native chancers, resurrections, and returns is located near the Skin Dip at Half Moon Bay. The word *azhetaa*, in the language of the *anishinaabe*, means to return or "go backwards." Sober whispers and natives return overnight from the past. Naturally, his stories and survivance ceremonies are reversals of the ordinary. For instance, he walks and talks backwards to reach that ecstatic moment of creation, and once there, in his backward stories, he turns the dead around on the road of absence. The actual resurrection of the native chancers was an elusive mosaic of tricky backward stories.

Cloud Burst was convinced that the backward stories of the undertone shaman would resurrect the native chancers in the museum. The solar dancers drove into the resurrection center with three bloody heads in a plastic bucket and expected to drive back that same night with a minivan of new natives. They wondered who the chancers might be on their return.

Pocahontas, shouted Bad Mouth.

You know, said Knee High.

Geronimo is a chancer, said Injun Time.

Chief Joseph, said Touch Tone.

Wovoka, said Fine Print.

Crazy Horse, man, said Fast Food.

Ishi is my chancer, said Token White.

Cloud Burst promised the solar dancers that many natives would return with each sacrifice, but they soon learned that resurrections were one head at a time, and that meant more sacrifices of the faculty.

Man, who are they, shouted Bad Mouth.

You know, said Knee High.

Chancers are newcomers, whispered Sober.

Not to me, said Fine Print.

Out of the past, whispered Sober.

Bad Mouth hated whispers. Mutters and mumbles she could bear, but never the hints and hisses of conversations. Whispers are white fakery, she shouted the first time she heard the undertone shaman. Later, however, she almost broke into a whisper when she saw the red worms clean the heads in minutes.

Cloud Burst mounted the three heads on the rim of the great cistern at the resurrection site. Blue Welcome held a pathetic pout. Snow Boy was caught in a scare, and the provost wore a mask of pain and misery. Token White turned away, haunted by the eyes of the dead heads. The three heads were cast in mortal stares.

The actual dissection of the three bodies never bothered the solar dancers, but the *miskwaa moose*, those nasty red worms, teased their scorn and sense of *wiindigoo* sacrifice. The worms were mutant flesh eaters, and thousands of them slithered in a clinch at the bottom of a converted cistern.

Fine Print winced and almost fainted at the edge of the cistern, as the worms reached out and hissed at the solar dancers. Sober whispered a few words to his three resurrection tyros and suddenly a bolt of lightning struck the tangle of worms. The flesh eaters bounced and slithered in wide circles, and even the solar dancers shivered from a mild shock. They moved back from the cistern.

The Mikawi Generator, an electrical machine, created the lightning and was somehow connected to the resurrection of native chancers. The thick copper wires, tied to the giant insulators overhead, purred and shivered with a wild blue light. Sober directed the lowest power of the machine on the cistern to tease the worms. Token White said he held back the actual sound of thunder for the resurrection of the chancers in the nearby Skin Dip.

Sober murmured a few lines from *Romeo and Juliet*, "How oft, when men are at the point of death, Have they been merry, which their keepers call, A lightning before death!" Shakespeare borrowed that idea from native shamans. The metaphor teases the return of the spirits at death, a moment of resurrection, as in the lightning of native chancers. Sober told the solar dancers that the word *mikawi* means, in *anishinaabe*, "to regain consciousness," and he was the master of native reversions and comebacks. The solar dancers wore their feathers and bright ribbons in preparation for a lightning before death, the return of the chancers.

That night a thick ocean fog rushed over the hills and shrouded the resurrection site. The solar dancers circled and taunted the three heads perched on the rim of the cistern. Sober whispered the order to the solar dancers and one by one the heads were pushed into the pit of red worms.

Pontius Booker was at the absolute end of his provostry. His bloody body parts had been thrown to the mountain lions, and then the last mask of his misery was devoured by red worms. They slithered into his nostrils and ate out his eyes. Token White told me that his ears were raised and carried to the side by the mass of worms, as if they were a cistern delicacy. The head of the provost, once packed with sixty years of memories and linguistic mappery, was eaten clean in minutes.

Snow Boy landed on the back of his head, his wild hair spread out over the mass of worms. Token White said the worms ate his chin, cheeks, and nose from the inside. His face caved in and his eyes seemed to come alive as the red worms slithered out of his orbital bones. Token White was caught once more in the last wormy gaze of the bone man.

Blue Welcome was the last meal for the ferocious worms that night. Her head slouched to the side on the rim of the cistern. Fast Food pushed her chin upright and moved her closer to the worms. She was the last resurrection sacrifice and the solar dancers bickered over who would boot her into the cistern.

Man, over the side, shouted Bad Mouth.

You know, said Knee High.

Welcome to the worms, said Injun Time.

Clean bone lovers, said Touch Tone.

Cloud Burst beat the *wiindigoo* drum, an eerie sound at the
Azhetaa Center. The solar dancers circled the cistern and waved
their flashlights in cadence with the sound of the drum. Knee
High danced around the cistern several times in the dark and
then, with a wicked hiss, he ran toward the last head on the
rim and kicked so hard that he lost his balance and toppled
into the cistern. Slowly, he was drawn into the clutch of
worms with the head of Blue Welcome.

Token White was sickened by the worm gorge, and she was
haunted by the last wormy gaze of Snow Boy. The solar dancers
teased her loudly in the dark and flashed their lights into her
eyes. Bad Mouth mocked the gawky moves of the blonde and
then waited for her brother to do the same, but he was not at
her side.

Knee High reached for the rope in silence, but it was too
late. By the time the solar dancers realized that he was gone
and turned their lights on the cistern the red worms had eaten
his toes to the bone. Bad Mouth shouted and pulled on the
rope, but the ferocious worms had already eaten his pelvis,
penis, and stomach and had slithered inside his chest. As she
raised the rope the nasty worms devoured his arms and hands.
Only a few finger bones and bits of tendon stuck to the end of
the rope.

Knee High, moaned Bad Mouth.

Shoot the worms, said Injun Time.

Cut the rope, whispered Sober.

Cut the rope, shouted Cloud Burst.

Bad Mouth leaned over the edge, and the others shined
their lights on the gruesome scene. She might have joined her

brother if the solar dancers had not cut the rope and held her
back from the cistern. Token White had distracted the solar
dancers with her haunt and miseries over the gaze of Snow
Boy. She became the scapegoat, the blonde forever blamed for
the death of Knee High.

White bitch, shouted Bad Mouth.

Sober lowered a thick metal screen over the cistern once the
worms had devoured the last traces of flesh on the three heads
and the remains of Knee High. The screen protected the worms,
as the resurrection tyros released seventeen hungry crows from
a nearby cage. The crows cawed, pecked, bounced on the screen,
and scared the red worms back into their burrows and black
water mines at the bottom of the cistern. Then the screen was
rolled back so the crows could catch a few slow, bloated worms.

Bad Mouth circled the cistern that night and mourned the
remains of her brother. She whispered to his absence and hated
the hoarse sound of her own voice. The solar dancers teased
her to shout, to break the whispers of a griever, but she had
lost her voice over the gruesome death of Knee High. That
morning she climbed into the cistern and gathered his bones,
one by one, from his phalanges, tibia, femur, pelvis, and ver-
tebra to his ribs, scapula, clavicle, and skull. Meticulously, she
packed each small bone into a brown shopping bag. Knee
High was a runty bundle in the end, and his skull rode on the
top of the bag.

Sober mounted the three resurrection skulls on an insulated
turntable at the Skin Dip. Bad Mouth at first held back the skull
of her brother but then decided that he might be resurrected as
a native chancer. Each of the four skulls was exposed to several

bolts of lightning on the turntable. The charges created thin cracks in the bone, the signatures of the ancient ones.

Old Darkhorse prepared a caldron of natural dyes to age the four skulls so they could replace the native chancers in the museum. Mouthy hooked the skulls by the orbital bones and slowly submerged them into the simmering solution.

Knee High, my brother, muttered Bad Mouth.

Shout, shout, shouted Cloud Burst.

He's a chancer, said Fast Food.

Resurrect my brother, shouted Bad Mouth.

The solar dancers were relieved to hear her natural, nasty voice and shouted in cadence as they moved around the caldron. Mouthy increased the heat and the skulls bounced and tumbled over and over, a strange sound in the copper caldron. The dark solution boiled over the sides, stained the bench and window, and splashed on two solar dancers. Fast Food had several brown polka dots on his right ear, nose, and the back of one hand. Token White was marked with several brown stains on her cheeks, each the shape of a teardrop.

Fast Food scooped out a cup of the solution and, when it was cool enough, poured it over his arms and giant white feet. His hands and arms darkened, but the bright porcelain tone of his feet remained the same. The color would not take, even when he squeezed the stain between his toes.

The skulls were boiled for several hours, tumbled in hot sand, polished twice, and then dried in a kiln. Bad Mouth reached too soon and burned her fingertips on the tiny skull of her brother. She cried and shouted over his remains spread out larger than life on the red carpet in the Skin Dip.

Later that night the solar dancers drove back to the campus, entered the museum, removed four native chancers, and replaced them with the treated skulls. Old Darkhorse told me that no one would notice the absence of the native skulls, and he was right. Pontius Booker, Snow Boy, Blue Welcome, and Knee High were mounted on a tray in the cage near the bone bench. They waited to be studied by graduate students. The native chancers, in turn, were returned to the Skin Dip.

The Mikawi Generator created fierce bolts of lightning, and natural blue streamers shot out of the orbital bones of the rescued museum skulls. The chancers were raised by the light, an imagic moment of resurrection. The faces of the chancers, and their distant smiles, were liberated by the blue light, a native sense of presence over the turntable at the Skin Dip.

Token White told me that she soared over the solar dancers, a shaman in ecstatic motion with the chancers. She soared on the blue light that night. Twice their bright faces were at the window, and then the roar of thunder erased the chance. The thunder moved the earth and scared the solar dancers.

Sober secured the skulls of the native chancers and buried them in the cold sand on the beach near San Gregorio. Mouthy stacked driftwood and started a great fire over the skulls. Cloud Burst wailed and beat the *wiindigoo* drum for hours that night, and the solar dancers shouted the names of native chancers.

ROUND DANCERS

Trickster stories
are imagic moments,
holosexual moves
in many directions
at the same time,
and the sexual teases
are natural reason
in the gentle eye
of a hurricane
moving to the wild,
elusive margins.

ORIFICE HOURS

Professor Peter Roses arrived a few minutes late, as usual, walked to the center of the classroom, turned once in a circle, and then started his lecture. He was at his best in constant motion, a natural storier, and he never carried notes.

His stories and turns were counter to the clock, in the same direction as a hurricane. By turns he teased the characters of native literature and touched by eye and gesture every student in the circle. Several thousand students have visited his courses in the past decade to hear the stories of a literary round dancer. My circuit is natural reason, he said, and the center is a hurricane, a trace of my presence, nothing more.

The themes of his courses, native histories, literature, and postindian cultural studies were tricky lectures on the curve. His stories were overtures to a native presence and, by turns, reworded so that the students on the circuit related to a variation of his lecture. The students who praised his academic moves the most, especially the slender blondes, became known as his round dancers. Naturally, the solar dancers hated the round dancers. The solar dancers hissed and ranted on the margins, the round dancers smiled and teased the entire circuit at the center.

The New Agers on campus said my mentor was the whirling dervish of native studies. He teased the romance of *indians*, on the turn, and raged against the political wiles of victimry. His courses were always overcrowded. Most of his students were inspired by his anecdotes and tricky associations in literature, but the more conservative faculty considered his lectures a savage canon, in the carnal sense.

Pardone de Cozener, the overweight but elusive lecturer on law and casino politics, said my mentor was precarious, a disgrace to serious native studies. Clearly, his mutable measures were jealousy. Round Dance was named, after all, an academic sensation in several tourist brochures, along with the plaza bucket drummer, the silent polka-dot man, the ethnic tunnel vision mural, Sather Tower, Ishi Court, People's Park, Cody's Books, and Moe's Books on Telegraph Avenue. Last winter more than three hundred tourists watched his turns on native trickster stories. My stories turn, he crowed to the tourists on the circuit, in the eye of a native hurricane.

Round Dance, one of his campus nicknames, as you know, has teased hundreds of women, mostly blondes, into orifice-hours sex and then roused them to boast of *their* seduction. Round Dance, however, has never consummated sex in the center, as his lectures were conducted, but on the rim, the border, or against the wall. He conceded that the best sex was in the corner.

Cedarbird, sex is the verge, said Round Dance.

He told me that his lecture turns were to the center, the very eye of a hurricane, a centripetal motion that outmaneuvered the solar dancers, the curse of the evil *wiindigoo*, and manifest manners. His round dance lectures were tricky and restorative, more than the chancy balance of romantic native reason. The brain, the mind, and sex have no center, no balance, he said, because erotic stories are holosexual, an obvious tease of natural reason in the corner. By holosexual he meant the entire rouse and motion of sex, animal or human.

Stories are never that easy.

The motion is obvious, said Round Dance.

So, why corner sex?

Sex was not a lecture, he told me, but rather the last of an ecstatic, tricky tease, and the motion was centrifugal, away from the center to the outside, to the secure corners of an imagic, holosexual moment on the verge. Round Dance was my mentor, and he was never without a story. I was never sure, however, if he intended to be so ironic. Sometimes he seemed to discover the actual irony as he told the story. That, in a sense, was what he meant by the imagic moment of a story.

Watch my moves, said Round Dance.

He was much closer to the students when he lectured on the move, always closer on the turns. Likewise, he turned his back on every student several times in a lecture, time enough on the rounds for the students to turn away, mimic his tricky manner, and pretend to stand behind his words and gestures to the students on the other side of the circle. The audience was recreated by his moves.

Naturally, my native sense of presence is motion, and that, my friend, is the name of natural reason, said Round Dance. Trickster stories are imagic moments, holosexual moves in many directions at the same time, and the sexual teases are natural reason in the gentle eye of a hurricane moving to the wild, elusive margins.

Round Dance was my academic mentor on campus, and for that the solar dancers were wary of my moves. The emissaries noted that my stories were at the center of the war between the solar dancers and the round dancers. Actually, the solar dancers ranted against everyone. Cloud Burst and his ruck of fideistic wailers were at the hard heart of victimry.

Round Dance aroused blondes by his smile and tricky moves. The solar dancers hated him because he mocked their wicked crusade, and because he lectured that they were mere poseurs of victimry. The solar dancers are the worst of the simulated *indians*, not natives in the sense of natural reason or survivance stories.

Hildie Harridan, the new provost, despised him even more than the solar dancers. She was an ethnic faker and feminist by measured scorn who shared with the overcast solar dancers a rant resentment of men and their trickster stories.

Round Dance was the curiosa of the campus, and he was high on her list of faculty marked for termination. Harridan had to create the murky evidence, however, because the accusers that she treated and counted on were those who had been denied sex during his orifice hours. She was marked that semester by her own depravity and became the second provost to vanish on the campus.

Round Dance had sex with his blondes at least three times a week during his orifice hours. My office was next to his, and the partitions were very thin on the third floor. Other lecturers visited my office from time to time to hear the round dancers moan, groan, and shout over sex in the corner.

TERMINAL INDIANS

Round Dance turned counter to the common consensus of native studies, and boldly announced in his seminars that the solar dancers were fideistic and that *indians* were inventions. Terminal creeders, he said, and simulations of victimry. Seven blondes sat in the center of the seminar, close to their master round dancer and his every word, and several tourists were there, as usual, to see the academic hurricane in action. The solar dancers were there to haunt and hinder his lecture by their terminal creeds. Round Dance always turned their resentments into satire. Injun Time, for instance, once wore a medicine pouch around his skinny neck to catch a better grade in the seminar. Round Dance warned him in a whisper that native medicine turns back on the pretenders. The solar dancer ran for the door because he had cursed my mentor with blindness.

Hildie Harridan ordered the university police to monitor our courses in native studies. She resented the round dancers, as you know, and was determined to create enough evidence to terminate Round Dance. I never asked, but the provost and police must have read my scenes by way of the ethnic emissaries. Meanwhile, the solar dancers had been under surveillance since the provost and the others had vanished that semester. Bonnie Hammer, one of the police monitors, was blonde, and she actually became a wanton round dancer.

Blondes in uniform are ready to be teased, said Round Dance. She was a wild round dancer early in the morning, and we could hear her shouts of favor and consent, louder and with more promise than the others. Jealousy, as you know, was as much an orifice curse as the solar dancers and their victimry. Hammer was aroused by the ruse, a natural, erotic spy. My mission is to tease native reason, said Round Dance.

James Baldwin asserted in a lecture on campus that in so far as you are white, you are insignificant, said Round Dance. So, he said in motion, insofar as we are *indians,* we are significant inventions and simulars.

Stories create our memories and sense of a native presence, but the names given by others, the inventions of *indians,* are an absence, said Round Dance. Language, then, structures the way we see the world, and when that world is created outside of our stories, we become the tack of inventions, and without a sense of presence.

Man, why do you always talk about what white people think, shouted Bad Mouth. Time you start talking about what *indians* are thinking for a change.

Right, *indians* love mother earth.

Now you're talking.

Your mouth is on *indian* time, said Round Dance.

Perfectly, shouted Bad Mouth.

And now we turn to literature, he said in motion, but first, how many of you read the *indian* stories that were assigned for today?

Bad Mouth and most of the *indian* students in the seminar were sullen and looked down or toward the window to avoid eye contact. Round Dance turned several times in silence, and then he shouted that the oral tradition is the *indian* way.

You mock us, said Token White.

Man, *indians* are oral, shouted Bad Mouth.

Not when you read, said Round Dance.

I read some stuff, said Fast Food.

What stuff?

The best *indian* parts.

Name one part, said Round Dance.

Sure, the part when the white man gets what he's got coming to him, that's the part that I liked the best, said Fast Food. He licked his lips, tore open a bag of corn chips, and munched for the rest of the seminar.

Token White declared that she had read the stories but she wished that she had not because the *indian* author, she thought, made the tribal people look foolish. She wore earphones, as usual, and was listening to Johnny Cash.

Ira Hayes. . . .

Satire is native, said Round Dance.

No, satire is not sacred, said Token White.

Mother earth is a natural satire.

No, never, protested Token White.

Consider the Waste Mountain Reservation.

No real *indian* would ever make a native nation out of city garbage, said Token White. That story does not honor *indians* and their suffering on reservations.

Right, a satire of victimry, said Round Dance.

Shit, man, that trash never meant nothing to me, shouted Bad Mouth. No *indian* writer would ever trash his own people like that, and that's because we got an oral tradition.

And oral waste, said Round Dance.

Touch Tone said there were no auras in the stories, and that was how she knew the author was not a real *indian* who lived on a reservation. Real *indians* have auras, and you can see them even in stories.

When *indians* write, you know, *indians* write, said Injun Time. He smiled and touched the leather medicine pouch around his neck, as if to say his words were an inspiration, not a curse. And when *indians* read, *indians* read, and when this *indian* reads, he reads what he likes to read, and he likes the short stories about the trash shaman because he had a shit load of visions right here in the city. Injun Time was urban born, a poseur shaman, herbal healer, and, as you know, an ecstatic solar dancer.

Round Dance turned twice and burst into laughter. Injun Time, he said, when this *indian* reads, he reads, and when he listens, he listens, and he laughs when he hears an ironic story about trash shamans. Yes, and you better not let go of that medicine pouch around your skinny neck.

You read too much, said Injun Time.

Wanaki animishimo wanaki, chanted Round Dance. He teased the solar dancers with native words and, as he turned in the center, he intoned the word *wanaki* over and over. Bad Mouth was nervous and waved her hands in resistance. She could not bear the sound of his native chanty.

Man, talk straight, shouted Bad Mouth.

He's talking *indian,* said Fast Food.

Round Dance turned once and waved to the solar dancers on the margins, a summons to the center. Four skins were lost in the trash, poor things.

Four Skins dead and gone.

No, the solar dancers, not the puppet.

Eight solar dancers, shouted Bad Mouth.

Knee High is dead, said Token White.

Four men, four skins, said Round Dance.

Shit, man, you talk trash.

The *anishinaabe* word *wanaki* means to live in a place of peace, and *animishimo wanaki* means to dance away in a place of peace, said Round Dance. Now, dance away and show me a place of peace in the solar dance.

San Gregorio, said Token White.

Round Dance turned and started his lecture about the second story that was assigned in the seminar that day. Orion, he read in motion, is a town on the other side of a great wall in Oklahoma and a constellation in the celestial equator that shows a great hunter with a sword.

Many families lived behind the Great Wall of Orion. They were the descendants of famous hunters and western bucking-horse breeders. Like good horses, read the notice on the great red wall, proud people keep to themselves and their own breed, but from time to time we invite others to share our food and conversations.

Round Dance paused on the turn and pointed out that some-one had crossed out one letter and changed the word breed to greed on the great wall. Only a single letter, one sound, like savage to ravage, turned the value of that notice. How does the sound of that one word change the significance of the story?

Greedy whites, shouted Bad Mouth.

Insofar as you are white, said Round Dance.

Greedy lecture, said Token White.

Neither breed nor greed is insignificant.

What about savage and ravage?

Round Dance read in motion from *Bearheart: The Heirship Chronicles.* Belladonna Winter Catcher, who was conceived and born at Wounded Knee, South Dakota, knocked at the gate. She was traveling with Catholic bishop Omax Parasimo and several other native pilgrims in search of a place of peace. We are natives on the run with good memories and a thou-sand stories. Bishop Omax teased, open the gate and let us in or we will blow your house down.

He never said that, said Token White.

Belladonna read out loud the sign at the entrance. Listen to this, the mind is the perfect hunter and narcissism is just another word for separation. Terminal creeds are set free in a walled community.

The metal portcullis opened and several uniformed guards escorted the native pilgrims through the Great Wall of Orion. The pilgrims were searched, and the guards recorded information about birthplaces, education, politics, travels, diseases, and cultural experiences. The hunters and breeders then welcomed the pilgrims to share their stories about the world outside their community.

What are you talking about? asked Fast Food.

Man, talk sense, shouted Bad Mouth.

Belladonna was asked by the hunters and breeders to be the good-spirited speaker that night at dinner. She shivered, nervously touched the turquoise beads around her neck, and then said that she would talk about *indian* dreams and values. Round Dance turned once in silence and then he continued to read from the novel.

Speak up, speak up, shouted a breeder.

Man, shut the fuck up, shouted Bad Mouth.

My talk is about *indian* values, she said in a stronger voice. We are raised with values that shape our world in a much different light, not white. We are *indian* and that means we are the children of dreams and visions. Our bodies are connected to mother earth, our minds are in the clouds, and our voices are the sweet breath of the wilderness.

Yes, mother earth, said Token White.

My grandfather was a hunter, and he told the same stories about the hunt that you say is an *indian* value, said one of the hunters. So, what do you mean to say?

I am not a whiteman, said Belladonna.

Man, you said it right, shouted Bad Mouth.

We can see that you are not a man, said an older woman, a hunter, but please show us how you are different, as you say, from a whiteman.

My blood is not white, said Belladonna.

Never, never white, shouted Bad Mouth.

Round Dance turned toward the blondes and then read another scene from *Bearheart*. We are different because we are raised by very different values, said Belladonna. She touched the bright turquoise beads at her neck. Our parents treat us with respect as children. We are loved and never punished. We live in big families and never send our old people to homes to be left alone. So, these are some things that make me different from a whiteman.

We are the true people, said Token White.

Tell us more, said a hunter.

Shut up and listen, shouted Bad Mouth.

Tribal people seldom touch each other, said Belladonna. She folded her arms over her breasts. We do not invade the places and bodies of others, and we do not stare at people when we are talking either, because *indians* have more magic in their lives.

Wait a minute, hold on there, said a hunter with an orange beard. Why do you pretend to make me so much different from your *indians* and separate me from other people in the world?

Belladonna speaks the truth, said Fine Print.

Tell me, why do you use that word *indian* in our presence? asked the hunter. Who are these people you name the *indians*, and where are they?

She talks for me, said Touch Tone.

And if you speak for all *indians* how can there be any truth
in what you say? asked the hunter. What have *indians* done in
this world?

The earth is our mother, said Belladonna.

Mother earth is a metaphor, said Round Dance.

The whiteman is evil, shouted Bad Mouth.

Raped mother earth, said Injun Time.

Round Dance turned in silence, and then he pointed to the
tourists standing near the door. He asked the tourists, the
hunter is here and he wants to know what the word *indian*
means. So, what does it mean?

You ask a tourist? shouted Bad Mouth.

Belladonna knows, said Token White.

Get back to the *indian* story, said Fast Food.

You must be stupid if you need help with the meaning of
the word *indian* and who we are in this world. Listen, an *indian*
is a member of a tribe and a person who has *indian* blood, said
Belladonna.

But what is *indian* blood?

She just told you, stupid, shouted Bad Mouth.

Our blood is not white, said Token White.

So, *indians* must be some modern invention, said the hunter
with the orange beard. Tell me, how is your invention any different from the *indians* we invented all over the world and
right out back on mother earth, the same mother you polluted
with everyone else?

Man, that's white shit, shouted Bad Mouth.

We invented you and that must be why you hate us so much,
because you were taken in by the same invention, shouted the

hunter. So, an *indian* is an *indian* because he thinks, speaks, and believes he is an *indian*, is that right?

Belladonna, you tell him, said Fine Print.

Mister hunter, what difference does the word *indian* make when I tell you from my heart that I have always been proud to be a true *indian*? My people are proud to speak the sacred language of mother earth, said Belladonna.

Man, that's great, shouted Bad Mouth.

Please continue, said a tourist.

Well, as I was saying, *indians* are closer to mother earth, to the very heart and energy of the woodlands and mountains and plains and rivers, said Belladonna. We are not a vicious people like the whites, who took everything and then wounded our mother earth.

Miss Belladonna, when you use the plural pronoun, asked a woman hunter with short white hair, does that mean that you are talking for all *indian* people?

Shit, man, shut up, shouted Bad Mouth.

Fine Print leaned into the circle, moved his mouth in silence for a few minutes, and then demanded an end to the story. What's all this nonsense about the pronouns of invention anyway?

Nothing but a story, said Round Dance.

Please, more, more, said a tourist.

Yes, most of them, said Belladonna.

Then, would your wild pronoun for *indians* include the ancient natives who built irrigation systems in the desert, and how about the western fishing tribes, the old tribes, the tribes that burned down their houses in potlatch ceremonies? Would they be the same *indians* as the American Indian Movement?

I have nothing more to say, thank you for the meal, said Belladonna. She sat down and several hunters and breeders touched her on the shoulders as they passed. She does not want to debate her ideas, said the hunter with the orange beard. They waited in silence, the hunters, breeders, blondes, solar dancers, and tourists.

Round Dance turned in silence.

Mother earth is precious to me, said Belladonna. Living is hearing the wind and speaking the languages of animals, and soaring with eagles in magic flight. I speak of the earth and the power comes to me in the words, and my *indian* blood gives me the strength to live and deal with evil. Suddenly the mood changed and the hunters and breeders cheered her stories.

Right on, *indian*, said a breeder.

Yes, right on, sister, said Token White.

The skins win, said Touch Tone.

Wait, there's more, said Round Dance.

Now is the time to present this child of mother earth with our special dessert, said the hunter with the orange beard. We have a tradition to honor some of our visitors with homemade dessert.

Please, no dessert, said Belladonna.

Give it to me, said Fast Food.

Now, now, you cannot turn down the hunters and breeders who listened to your stories over dinner, said the hunter. This is a proud *indian* dessert, how could you refuse our home-made cookies?

The hunters and breeders arose to cheer, whistle, and shout their approval when the cookies were served to Belladonna.

Bishop Omax Parasimo and the other visitors at dinner were suspicious of the excessive praise, the sudden, strange energies.

Man, weird hunters, shouted Bad Mouth.

Savage to ravage, said Round Dance.

Not really, said a breeder. You see, when there are no answers and no humor, then the stories are terminal creeds, and the good hunters and breeders treat terminal creeds as the bitter end of reason behind the Great Wall of Orion.

Serve the dessert, said a tourist.

Cookies, more cookies, said Fast Food.

Your stories of *indians* are terminal creeds, said a hunter, and *indians* are perfect victims when they lose their sense of humor and irony. Racial pride is the absence of irony, and separations are terminal stories.

Man, you made that up, shouted Bad Mouth.

Solar dancers are proud, said Token White.

Round Dance smiled and turned in silence. He looked around the seminar room and then continued to read in a much louder voice to the end of the story.

Belladonna, alas, did not eat sweets, but she was gracious to the hunters and breeders. The executioners cheered as she nibbled on the sugar cookie. Her cheeks turned red, and her tongue tingled from the tartness. The cookie, you see, was covered with a granulated time-release alkaloid poison that would soon dissolve. The poison cookie was the special dessert for racial narcissists, said the hunter with the orange beard.

My Belladonna, moaned Token White.

Sick hunters, said Fast Food.

Man, evil story, shouted Bad Mouth.

The hunters and breeders have poisoned hundreds of visitors over the years for their terminal creeds. Most of them were terminal creed *indians* who had been invited to dinner and stories behind the Great Wall of Orion. Belladonna savored the last crumbs of the poison cookie.

Just desserts, shouted a breeder.

ACOUSTIC SHAMAN

Conk Browne was an elevator shaman who had been invited to teach a seminar that spring semester on native transmotion and visionary sovereignty. Truly, she had several visions on elevators, became a notable motion mechanic, and then located the bones of Pocahontas at Indian Queens in Cornwall.

Pocahontas was always at her side, posed in a wide ruffed collar and fancy court costume, based on the engraved portrait by Simon de Passe. Conk had a huge portrait of the princess mounted on the wall in her office. The same portrait was created in a stained glass window at St. George's Parish Church at Gravesend in England. Pocahontas is my perfect monarch of native sovereignty, said Conk.

Round Dance, of course, was eager to contribute his bones for discovery. Daily, he teased the origin of her native nickname, a hair style, a nose, a conch, and a conk on the head. Naturally, his tease was to the very conk of sex, but she would have nothing to do with his bones or the round dancers. Nothing, but to overhear and descry the sound of his bones in erotic motion, a motion that moved the portrait of the princess.

Pocahontas was the precise cause of her seminar on visionary motion, not sex, but the actual motion of the round dancers
in the next office changed the content of her course at the
university.

Round Dance was overheard in motion on both sides of his
office. Conk on one side, and me on the other. We heard the
gentle rise of his voice, the erotic summons, the entrance tease,
and then the moans to motion and the heavy breath of his
many blondes. When the couch in the corner of his office hit
the wall the rush was on, and no one could avoid the excite-
ment of round dancer sex, not even the portrait of Pocahontas.

The Mendelian race was heard all the way to the elevator at
the end of the hallway. I waited for the wild motion, the hesi-
tation, and then the absolute pitch of orgasms. He told me that
once or twice he pretended to have sex, pounded on the wall,
and wailed only to torment Conk and her peculiar aunt, the
private investigator named Tulip Browne.

Conk had a vision of an elevator on the reservation that
came true in a condominium in the city. She was eight years
old, the vision conked out four years later, and that vision of
motion, the natural rise of an automatic elevator, gave her an
unshakable nickname and a truly great profession.

The vision of an elevator came true and then conked near
the seventh floor of the condominium. The electrical power
had failed in a thunderstorm. She was alone, stranded in the
dark for more than an hour, but the experience proved that
her vision was greater than her fear of silence. The elevator
became her sense of presence.

Conk traveled with her aunt, an exotic woman who hated men and investigated notable crimes and rode on the elevators in grand hotels. Later, in a technical school, she studied the actual motion of elevators, the motors, gears, cables, weights, hydraulics, and the electronics. She learned how to hear the signature sounds of elevators, the murmurs, shivers, shudders, clicks, and slow breaks, and how to imagine the stories of mechanical secrets. Conk became an acoustic shaman and the best motion mechanic in the world. She could sense mechanical conditions and was excited by the elusive undertones of elevators in motion, and much like her aunt, she was disconcerted by the actual motion and sounds of sex.

Conk told me that her aunt, the private investigator, taught her how to create stories about motion, the moods, manners, and aims of characters on elevators. She told stories about silence, and considered a career as a detective, but instead became an acoustic shaman and motion mechanic.

Tulip owned a luxurious condominium on the seventeenth floor surrounded by miniature windmills. She was taken with the sounds of natural power, but not men, and certainly not the pageant moans of blondes or the ecstasies of round dancers that her niece endured at the university.

Tulip worried about her niece, abused in her first semester of teaching by the constant heave and beat of sex, so she built two windmills in the windows of her office. The great copper blades whirred on the ocean wind, a perfect balance of natural, meditative sounds that obscured the noise of the round dancers.

Conk told me about her second vision at Claridge's Hotel in London. Hired to examine the lofty elevators there, she heard more than the signatures of class and acoustics of motion. She heard the lonesome stories of her sister Pocahontas. Yes, she said her sister, and decided then and there to find her bones. Conk came by air, the princess by sea, as you know, and they met in numinous motion as sisters on a grand elevator three centuries later. She told some of these same stories at a faculty meeting at the start of the semester and caused a trivial silence of uncertainty. Natives, in positions to promote the academic cause of visions, were bored by the actual, mundane stories of visions.

Call me John Rolfe, said Round Dance.

Not in my story, said Conk.

Bones have rights, said Pardone de Cozener.

Naturally, the faculty laughed, but the misdoubts about the acoustic shaman were never pardoned. The native dead might return, but academic doubts were not repealable. Actually, the round dancers teased each other on the elevators about the tricky presence of their relatives, Pocahontas, Metacom, Geronimo, Crazy Horse, Sitting Bull, Standing Bear, Gertrude Bonnin, Charles Eastman, and Ira Hayes.

Pocahontas was anxious and faint with a fever as she boarded the *George* anchored at Tower Steps on the River Thames, said Conk. A short time later her sister was taken ashore and died at Gravesend. Conk told me that she was there in a vision at her burial near the church of Saint Marie's, but then the stories ended when the elevator reached the lobby.

Conk was ready to search for her stolen bones, but her sister did not return to the elevators at Claridge's in Mayfair. So, she visited the statue of her sister in the garden at St. George's Parish Church at Gravesend. Conk said she cleaned her moccasins, polished her bronze hands, and told stories about elevator visions. Later, she was inspired by the image of her sister who moved in the light of the stained glass windows of the church.

Pocahontas was the Indian Queen, said an old man, the verger of the church. Conk was told that a fisherman bought the bones of the princess for good luck and then returned to his home at St Ives in Cornwall. Conk was on the train the very next day. The Penzance Scenic Railway ran along the coast of Carbis Bay to the station at St Ives.

The mighty fuchsia trees had grown over the steep path on the rise to the Porthminster Hotel. The elusive stonechats were in the thickets, and the herring gulls shouted overhead. Pocahontas might have walked on the very same ancient stones. Conk said she could sense her presence, but then her sister vanished once more as the porter opened the doors to the hotel.

Conk, as you might imagine, was drawn to an old elevator in the hotel. Marryat and Scott of London built the gated elevator in the center of the grand stairway sometime after the hotel was founded in 1894. She described the brass fittings with great care. Naturally, most of my colleagues were bored to savagery by the elevator details.

I was charmed by her stories and truly moved by her elevator passion and memory. Conk created an original native sense of presence, a humane and numinous history. Pocahontas must have been there, at our faculty meeting, as she was forever in motion, and she must have been aware of her own presence in the elevator stories.

Conk was amused and then turned toward the windows in the conference room. Pocahontas is with me now, she said twice in a murmur. I heard a rush of wind, and the blinds rattled, a haunting sound, but nothing more hinted at the presence of her sister.

Round Dance studied her gestures, her eyes in the bright light, the lusty turn of her lips, the spread of her thighs, the angle of her feet, and once more he boldly invited the acoustic shaman to a round dance. Pardone de Cozener, the elusive lecturer on law and casino politics, read his mail, and the others pretended to listen to her story.

Conk was truly animated by her stories of discovery. She said the hotel manager, an older man with enormous, rough hands, had no idea what was wrong with the elevator. She cleaned the electrical contacts and brakes and had the entire system serviced and in order by dinner. Pocahontas, the manager told her, turned out to be an unlucky name in St Ives. She was aboard the *Amelia* with Barnabas Stevens and James Penberthy when the boat was lost at sea in September 1934.

The acoustic shaman told many other stories of transmotion that afternoon, but most of the faculty had escaped as the memory train arrived in St Ives. Only two lecturers remained to listen by the time she had repaired the elevator at the Porthminster Hotel. Round Dance was there for the humor and chance of sex. I was there for the same chance, and for the visionary stories. Conk aroused me, but not as a round dancer.

She was a healer not a hunter, and she teased the vision of the bear and crane in me.

St Ives might have been her town, she told me, if only there had been more elevators. Conk heard many stories about the men of the sea there, as she had heard many stories about men of the lakes on the reservation. Men, water, and women, she said, are the great trickster stories of creation, and once in motion, men have never been at peace in their stories. She said the loves of men were an absence, always adrift, once at sea for women, and once moored, a passion for the sea.

Conk listened to the motion of scenes, a natural meditation, and learned from her aunt how to create stories of motion. She could hear and see motion in every word. Tulip encouraged me to pretend that our reservation was on an elevator and that everything native was in motion, she said, and that was the start of my visual memories. Conk announced that the best memories of motion are the best stories, and then she told me about the night her mother vanished on the reservation. The story, at first, seemed to have no obvious connection to chancers or to St Ives.

Samuel Beckett came to mind again, another narrative voice in motion, the cries of the elevator. "Each tree had its own cry, just as no two whispered alike, when the air was still," he wrote in *Malone Dies*. "I heard afar the iron gates clashing and dragging at their posts and the wind rushing between their bars. There was nothing, not even the sand on the paths, that did not utter its cry."

Conk said her mother was a solitary person, so no one really worried about where she might have gone. Then, several days later, her father and other relatives started to search in the obvious places, the church mission, the outlet store, and the casino. She was not a drinker, but sometimes she would listen to big band music on the jukebox and dance alone at the nearby resort.

My father said nothing about the ice house, she said, because my mother told him never to bother her there, not for any reason, but he always found some reason to visit the tiny house on the lake. He would arrive with stories about the weather, the dogs, family gossip, and each time my mother sat in silence, said Conk. She sat in an aluminum lawn chair and read novels, and she always had two fishlines tied to her wrist. The novels came first, of course, even when a fish tugged at the line. Conk told me that she could hear the fish cut the water just before they took the bait.

Conk said her mother was last seen walking in the heavy snow near the water tower on the day she vanished, but no one could remember in what direction. She was not at the ice house. Finally, the family reported that she was missing. The county sheriff came by two days later and pretended that he was concerned. He wrote her name in his spiral notebook, but he was not really serious because natives have vanished forever on the reservation.

Conk envisioned her mother in motion, as a scene in a story. First she listened and created her mother as a visionary presence, in transmotion, and then actually discovered her at the public library in a nearby town. She was in the corner reading *Love Medicine* by Louise Erdrich. I could hear my mother turn the pages of that novel at a great distance, said Conk.

Pocahontas was in motion, a presence and, at the same time, she was an absence. Conk listened to many stories about her sister and then tried to envision her in St Ives. She browsed in a used bookstore near the harbor, for instance, and asked the owner, a joyous woman with no front teeth, about her sister. Pocahontas, said the woman, was rescued by a curious survivor of the marvelous land of Lyonesse. Trevelyan of Basil is his name, and he once lived in Lann Stefan near the Bodmin Moor.

Pocahontas must have heard the same stories about her bones, because that night on the hotel elevator she told her sister the true stories. Conk envisioned the scenes. My bones were stolen from the grave near Saint Marie's in Gravesend, she said, and later sold to a fisherman, but none of me was ever lost at sea.

Conk looked past me, out the window, as she heard the voice of her sister, a natural presence. The fisherman was worried that my bones might have brought bad luck to others, she said, so he buried my remains near Indian Queens in Cornwall.

Conk recovered her sister's bones on a cold and misty morning. Pocahontas was buried in a shallow, unmarked grave, covered with heavy stones. Naturally, the metal box had rusted, but the bones had been tightly wrapped in layers of thick leather. Only the tiny bones of her hands and feet, a fibula, and both patellae were lost. Conk cleaned each bone, polished the crania, and bound her sister in black velvet. Later, she sealed the bones in a titanium chest. Conk never again left her sister alone.

Sober Browne and the solar dancers were eager to resurrect the remains and stories of Pocahontas at the Azhetaa Center at Half Moon Bay. Conk was curious about the resurrection center, but she refused to consider her sister a native chancer. Pocahontas is a princess, not a chancer, she said, and she will never be buried again, not even by a shaman, and certainly not by strangers on the beach at San Gregorio.

HOLOSEXUAL MOTION

Blondes stimulate my best research, and holosexual motion, and the entire turns, rush, and tricky nose of sex, are a native tease, said Round Dance. Cedarbird, he said, my holosexual motion is a version of native resurrection, the rise of lust, and that wild chance of conception. He was in a position to know more than anyone, because he has teased so many blondes in the corner of his office. Several times a week, and sometimes more than once a day, the moans and thunder of the couch against the wall overcame the constant meditative whirs of the windmills.

Pardone de Cozener said my mentor was a roundabout talker with too much motion. Maybe so, but the chicken plucker and casino panderer always happened by my office in time to hear the afternoon round dances. Pardone would rather listen at a distance, the base practice of moot sex. He tried to use the round dance to advance his position in native studies, but his servile, insincere manner and beastly leer only perverted the stories.

Tulip surprised her niece one afternoon in her seminar. Conk had just presented a comparative description of shamanic ecstasies and the mental dissociations of schizophrenia when her aunt entered the classroom and took a seat at the seminar table. I came along and was part of the event. The students, of course, were more than eager to be distracted and entertained by the stories of a famous native detective.

Tulip Browne, my aunt, is one of the greatest sleuths in the history of native sovereignty, said Conk. She has investigated and collected stories of crimes in countries all over the world. Conk was touched by the surprise, and turned the seminar over to her aunt.

Name a country, said Tulip.

China, said a student.

Tulip paused, looked out the window, and then started her stories. Zhou Enlai University in Tianjin is a culture of concession memories, lost relatives, and the painted faces of classical opera scenes, said Tulip. Egas Zhang, the director and shadow cadre in charge of the foreigners on the campus, invited me to investigate the subversive activities of a native teacher named Griever de Hocus.

How did they know you? asked a student.

Communist Party? asked another student.

China Browne, my cousin, was at the university doing research on Alicia Little, the past president of the Natural Foot Society, said Tulip. Little was a missionary who organized the opposition to footbinding in China. My cousin was fascinated by the subject and earned a nickname for her trouble. She told the cadre about me, and the State Department endorsed my services. I had carried out many secret investigations for our embassies in Europe and Asia.

Did she know Griever?

China had received several critical letters from Griever, and later she learned that he had vanished on an ultralight airplane, said Tulip. Slyboots, our cousin, built ultralights on the reservation and hoped the cadre might order thousands of them and make him rich and famous, but that's another story.

Griever was known on the campus as a holosexual clown, a native cousin of the monkey king, because of his lusty moves and tricky stories. A few faculty and most of the students were charmed by his trickster maneuvers, but the cadre who actually ran the university were not amused by his behavior, and they resented his influence on students.

Egas told me that Griever came back from the street market on his very first day in the country with blood and feathers on his shoes and whistling "The Stars and Stripes Forever." Griever de Hocus, it turned out, had liberated every caged chicken at the street market.

What did he do with them? asked a student.

Actually, he bought the chickens, and in a sense freed them from bondage and certain death, but most of the chickens ran right back to their cages. Griever disrupted the market for several hours, and that, the actual social disorder, bothered the cadre more than anything, said Tulip. Later, he decorated his face and dressed like a monkey king from the opera, *Havoc of Heaven*. Truly, the students and many others loved his performances, but the severe cadre were determined to send the trickster home.

So, why was that a crime? asked a student.

Griever was under suspicion for crimes against the state, and the punishment for that was death, said Tulip. Simply owning a road map was a serious crime at the time. Egas and the other cadre wanted to avoid an international incident, partly because the trickster was native. Griever was a popular teacher, but they could not allow his disruptive behavior to go unpunished. So, they invited me to conduct a secret investigation.

Tell the students what happened, said Conk.

Griever, the faculty, students, and practically everyone else in the country were awakened every morning to "The East is Red." China has only one time zone, so the national music was broadcast at the same time across the country.

One morning, however, the patriotic marches had changed, said Tulip. "The Stars and Stripes Forever" and "Semper Fidelis" were broadcast across the campus. Griever had located the transmission center one early morning, changed the tapes, and invaded the country with the rousing music of John Philip Sousa. You can imagine how startled many people were, especially the elders who did their daily tai chi to the music. The cadre considered his act a crime against the People's Republic of China.

Egas remembered that the trickster had whistled the same tune when he liberated the chickens, the day he returned from the market with blood and feathers on his shoes. Egas called me to investigate, but in the end the government ignored my report, said Tulip. My concern was not state disorder, and certainly not the behavior of tricksters and monkey kings, but rather the ordinary security of the transmission center on campus. Practically every door and drawer in the country was chained and double padlocked, but not windows. Griever borrowed a ladder from a nearby construction site and climbed through an open window early in the morning. Clearly, the cadre were more interested in symbolic locks than security systems.

Tulip's story foreshadowed what happened a few weeks later at the University of California. She was contracted by the university police to investigate the sexual activities of my mentor and the round dancers in native studies. The police, however, were caught short by the evidence. Many blondes, one solar dancer, and the provost were recorded, as you know, in the corner with my mighty mentor, Round Dance.

The police pretended to be surprised by the report, but they would never use the audio or video tapes as evidence against the provost. So, the round dance tapes were stored away, but not for long. The solar dancers stole the tapes and broadcast the acoustic evidence on emergency loudspeakers across the campus. That was a day to remember in native studies. Griever would have hailed the transmission as a patriotic irony. The sexual moans and shouts of that nasty provost were heard in every corner of the campus. The faculty, for the most part, considered the broadcast poetic justice, a masterly act of vengeance.

Racy early warning system, said a student.

Never mind, said Conk.

My faculty office was on one side of the round dance corner, as you know, and the whir of windmills was on the other. The whir, in fact, became the meditative, ambient sound on the round dance tapes and actually enhanced the erotic quality of the productions.

Tulip bored two holes in the wall near the round dance corner, inserted a miniature video camera in one hole, and mounted a voice activated microphone in the other. The tapes recorded the teases, sex chatter, moans, and the round dance rush of seventeen blondes, one solar dancer, and the provost. Most of the faculty could not imagine that the provost was even capable of sex, much less of a wild encounter, but there she was, on video tape, a rather emaciated, peevish creature mounted for the round dance. The bony provost seemed pathetic at the start, but clearly she was moved by the heat. Round Dance told me he was aroused by her neurotic, evil radiance, and he knew the corner scenes were recorded. Hildie became an erotic crone, and the wild motion of her last thrusts were obscure on the video tape.

Conk said the provost was depraved and more dangerous than the round dancers. Tulip observed that the provost was obsessed with the puissance of men, and overcame manly warrants with the beat of nasty sex. They were both right, of course, but my report to the emissaries, as you know, pointed out that the provost was more aroused by the perverse absence of men, and the resentment of sexual fantasies, than by any testy presence. Hildie took the erotic teases of the round dance to be an aesthetic perversion on university property. What she truly needed was a windmill, maybe several, said Tulip.

Token White was the one solar dancer caught on the round dance tapes. She was angular, bright, sweaty, and shy, an ecstatic murmurer, in contrast to the wild, withered provost in the corner. Round Dance told me that her timid, backward moves were very erotic, but he was more aroused by the natural, sweet scent of her boyish body. The video tapes show him licking her arms, legs, neck, sucking other parts, and rutting in her blond crotch. Token White was obsessed with holosexual lust and shivered for hours after an encounter in the corner. Naturally, she became his secret, prima round dancer.

Seasons of My Heart. . . .

Token White never forgave the solar dancers, who broadcast the round-dance tapes on campus, and she hated the provost. She contained her silent rage and savage jealousy for almost three weeks, and then sacrificed the provost at her own desk. Hildie was immolated, an incredible act of vengeance.

I Walk the Line. . . .

The provost was cornered by her own resentments and abused the round dance by envy. Actually, the round dance was a tricky, erotic liberation from the academic perversions of mind, body, and aesthetic resentments, but she was dry and clumsy with emotions and could not bear the tease of native survivance. Hildie might have been aroused by mere shame, even the awkward pleasure of lusty indiscretions, but she was too hounded by resentment, scorn, and jealousy. When the round dance tapes were broadcast across the campus and a website was created to post nasty provost stories, she secretly consorted with the solar dancers, who hated sex and natural reason. Hildie, who arose out of ethics and religious studies, became the provost of academic perversions, envies, and victimry.

Token White outraged the solar dancers. She was the blonde mole on the round dance tapes, an ironic betrayal of perversity. Bad Mouth convinced the provost to block the return of Ishi's brain, deny the ceremonial reburial of his ashes on the campus, and other acts of revenge against Token White. The provost, in turn, incited the solar dancers to vex and bewilder the round dancers in native studies, but not Pardone de Cozener. Hildie was an evildoer but she ha ¹ no sense of *wiindigoo* violence. The demise of my mentor was much more important to the provost than her own wanton giveaway.

The solar dancers used the conspiracy with the provost to carry out their villainy. They stole the ashes and brain of Ishi and the bones of Pocahontas.

Round Dance continued his holosexual lectures on the curve, the tourists arrived on schedule, and he held the usual orifice hours with blondes. Token White, however, was always on his mind, and he seemed to be more astounded by the irony than the rest of the faculty. She was, after all, one of his many blondes. Somehow, he was never the subject of the round dance tapes, and though he was asked many times, he never revealed how he was able to hold an erection with the provost on top. Always, his holosexual scenes were a native mien of survivance.

Round Dance is a carnal mutant, said Cozzie.

The emissaries, in one of those rare responses to my reports, wrote that the precise moment of sexual ecstasy might be the actual outcome of decadence and perversion. The ruins of the soul arouse as many people as the tease of trickster stories, and that irony must be at the heart of natural reason.

The solar dancers were evermore at war with blondes and round dancers, the resentments of terminal creeders against the erotic, holosexual tease of a trickster. The stories of survivance, as you know, outmaneuvered their terminal creeds, villainy, and victimry.

CRONE CREMATION

Token White readied her sacred Yahi bow, nocked an arrow with a tiny explosive device set in the obsidian point, and waited for the provost to lean over her desk near the window.

Hildie was sacrificed because she betrayed the remains and memory of Ishi. The provost had resisted the petition to return his brain for cremation and reburial in a ceremonial vault in Ishi Court at the University of California.

Ishi was rescued by anthropologists almost a century ago and lived in the Museum of Anthropology. Ishi was my brother, he died in my arms, and his sacred blood is my blood, said Token White. That eternal moment, she envisioned, was on March 25, 1916. The Yahi were hounded to their death in the late nineteenth century by savage miners and state bounty hunters. Ishi was one of the last storiers of a distinctive culture of native sovereignty.

Ishi was cremated and his ashes were placed in a niche at Mount Olivet Cemetery in Colma, California. Recently, his preserved brain, which had been excised during an autopsy, was discovered in a jar at the Smithsonian Institution. Robert Fri, director of the National Museum of History, reported that "Ishi's brain will be returned to his closest living relatives, the Yana people of the Redding Rancheria and Pit River Tribe," in accordance with the Native Graves Protection and Repatriation Act. "The Yana will then determine how to proceed with a proper burial."

Token White was disheartened and very angry that his brain would not be returned to the campus. Her pain and silent rage turned vindictive when she learned that the provost had not only resisted the return of his brain and opposed a reburial on campus but had actually concealed the theft of the brain. Later, as an act of incredible vengeance and perverse, poetic justice, the brain of the provost was cremated as she leaned over her own desk.

Hildie worked late that night in her office on the second floor of the administration building on campus. The fogbank was held at sea, the bay was clear at dusk, and a warm wind raised the leaves on campus. The provost opened the window, and for a few minutes, she watched the students outside the main library.

Token White had waited in a classroom across the way from the provost for that very moment of vulnerability. She locked the door and raised her bow in the dark. The orange glow of the sunset lingered behind the administration building. The smooth arrow, a hazel stick rolled over heated stones, had been soaked in poisonous, reactive phosphorus.

Hildie was at ease for the first time since the round dance tapes had been broadcast on campus. She had weathered the acrimony of the faculty and took cover in a conspiracy with the solar dancers. The round dance tapes were at hand, delivered that very afternoon, but actually the box contained an explosive chemical. Nothing seemed to bother her as she leaned over her desk, stacked high with the trivial documents of her provosty.

Token White was a shaman of archery. She envisioned the precise moment of creation, steadied her breath in meditation, braced her sacred bow as a hunter, and then released the arrow into an ancient presence, the muse of an absolute union with the provost. The sound was lost on the warm wind, and then the arrow pierced the provost in the neck. Hildie raised her hands as the obsidian point passed through her neck and exploded on the other side. Tiny pieces of the shattered stone cut her hands, neck, and face. The reaction of the phosphorus in the arrow set her hair afire, and when her head slumped forward the flames rapidly spread to the papers on her desk. A few minutes later chemicals in the box exploded and the office was ablaze, an inferno, and by the time the fire trucks arrived, the provost had been cremated at her desk. Only a few teeth and the case of her expensive wristwatch were found in the ashes.

CHICKEN PLUCK

Cloud Burst
and the solar dancers
are the victims,
the round dancers
are the erotic visionaries,
and our own
stinky chicken plucker
is the perfect clown
and scapegoat.
Now that, my friends,
creates the sacred
in native studies.

MÉTIS MAPPERY

Pardone de Cozener was a poseur, a creature of names, stains, and chicken feathers, but he had no native ancestors. Rather, he was a consort simulation who served the academic subversions of three provosts. He started out as a government mapper of reservations, a shy surveyor of many steads, and slowly he became a native by the association of obscure names.

Cozzie White Mouth, as he was known to the solar dancers, simulated his way with mappery, the invention of landscapes, and braced his solemn favors with chicken feathers on his sleeve. He learned to mention native names at strategic moments and won a fellowship to law school. Geronimo, Crazy Horse, Eastman, Standing Bear, Ishi, Riel, Means were some of the native names he announced with association stories. Cozzie had a tricky pose but he needed more color about his jowls and thighs to be persuasive. So, Old Darkhorse stained his skin a burnt cinnamon brown at the Half Moon Bay Skin Dip. Cozzie returns at least twice a year to even out the poseur tone.

Cozzie was hired as a lecturer on native law and sovereignty, and, in the past few years, he became an expert on casino gaming. He won on names and academic poses, but lost on reservation slot machines, and everyone knows he would rather be with his favorite chickens. Yes, as in fowl, cocks and hens. Twice a day, every day, he plucks away at his Paraday Chicken Pluck Center on Telegraph Avenue in Berkeley.

Cozzie was never a natural, so he conspired with the solar dancers only to overthrow the round dancers and take control of native studies on the campus. Actually, nothing could have been easier, as you know, but the way he went about the coup was so obscure that no one could figure out the scheme, the reactions, or counter moves. His notions of a native transnational constitution were elusive fusions of sovereignty and ethnic victimry. Several provosts heard his servile connivance but nothing ever changed in native studies. The faculty was bored by the conceit of fusions, and the students were already separated by the absolute metaphors of their own dances, solar or erotic.

The spurious mapper was a man of mass nouns, except for the breeds of chickens he plucked with rare passion. The nouns of his lectures, for instance, were common, massive, never precise or countable, such as some earth, truth, water, music, nation, wine, words, and fusions of sovereignty. Obviously, his mass nouns were elusive mappery. Truly, no one worried about his wacky maneuvers, but three provosts tried to exploit the division of native studies. Not only were his academic schemes inscrutable, but the solar dancers, inspired by the evil *wiindigoo*, sacrificed every provost who might have supported his moves against the round dancers. Cozzie, by the pluck of his chickens, was a common nouny.

The Faculty Club, he reminded me, was designed by the late, great architect, Bernard Maybeck. Cozzie was never more at ease than in the baronial presence of names. Notice the classical and medieval fusions that create an organic reach of redwood and natural plaster, he said as he pointed to the fireplace and overhead beams, neither of which were the material he named. Maybeck designed the Palace of Fine Arts in San Francisco, and Wyntoon for Phoebe Apperson Hearst, a country retreat on the McCloud River near Mount Lassen.

Ishi was hounded by bounty hunters. He was run out of that same part of the country, but notable names, not native histories, were always more important to Cozzie. He reasoned that Phoebe Hearst created a museum to honor natives. Who could have done more?

Crazy Horse, said Injun Time.

Ishi, said Token White.

Louis Riel, said Touch Tone.

Douse me, said Cozzie.

Man, you stink, shouted Bad Mouth.

Touch Tone once rented a room in a house in the hills that was designed by Bernard Maybeck. She was evicted, however, long before she heard the name of the architect. The owner, a cranky widow, discovered that she was native, dark and thick at the waist, she said, and told her to leave. Actually, the widow was terrified by the solar dancers, who peered in the windows.

Touch Tone earned her nickname at that house, said Cozzie. He never missed the chance association of names. She turned the eviction into vengeance and charged more than a hundred long-distance telephone calls to friends and relatives around the world. The solar dancers also charged many long-distance calls to native studies.

Touch Tone called, as she does at least once a year, the court in Regina, Saskatchewan, Canada. Why, she asks the clerk of court, did you kill my great, great, grandfather, Louis Riel? The clerk was polite but never answered the sentence, but the point was made. Touch Tone also called several prisons and told the guards to release the natives, especially Leonard Peltier. The conversations with her aunt in Hindustan, however, were the most expensive, because they were conference connections with her parents in South Dakota.

Louis Riel was a métis insurgent who was convicted of high treason in a feud of sovereignty, an immoral, political indictment by a colonial monarchy. Riel was a citizen of the United States, and yet he was tried under the Treason Act of Britain. Riel had established a métis government, but his army was defeated at Batoche, Saskatchewan.

Touch Tone read to the clerk of court the very same charges that her great, great grandfather had heard that morning in court. Riel was indicted for "not regarding the duty of his allegiance, nor having the fear of God in his heart, but being moved and seduced by the instigation of the devil as a false traitor against our said Lady the Queen." The trial opened on July 28, 1885, with the selection of six jurors. The prosecutor told the jurors that they were part of the "most serious trial that has probably taken place in Canada." Riel was asked by the judge if he was guilty or not guilty?

Man, not guilty, shouted Bad Mouth.

This is our realm, said Fast Food.

"I have the honor to answer the court I am not guilty," said Louis Riel. He was shackled with a ball and chain on his ankle. Riel had a great beard and wore a black frock coat, white shirt, and black cravat. "I am not guilty."

Riel is a solar dancer, said Token White.

Round dancer, said my mentor.

Man, never, never, shouted Bad Mouth

Touch Tone studied *The Strange Empire of Louis Riel* by Joseph Kinsey Howard and memorized several dramatic scenes from the script, *The Trial of Louis Riel,* by John Coulter. She continued her long-distance recitation, and every year for the past decade, the clerk of court has listened to the very end of what became a familiar story.

Louis Riel, a jury of "unexampled patience," has found you "guilty of a crime the most pernicious and greatest that man can commit," said Justice Richardson. "It is now my painful duty to pass the sentence upon you. And that is that you be taken now from here to the police guardroom at Regina, which is the gaol and the place from whence you came." Then, "you be taken to the place appointed for your execution, and there be hanged by the neck till you are dead." Riel was hanged a month later on November 16, 1885.

Riel is my brother, said Injun Time.

His name is ours, said Cozzie White Mouth.

Please call again, said the clerk of court.

"The trap opened and Riel's body plunged nine feet," wrote Joseph Kinsey Howard. "It quivered and swayed on the taut rope." A doctor felt for a pulse and said, "It beats yet, slightly."

SOLAR DIMENSIONS

Ransom Greene, the acting provost, invited Cozzie to a lunch meeting at the Faculty Club to discuss the future of native studies and the repatriation of native remains in the Phoebe Hearst Museum of Anthropology. The subject of native studies, students, faculty, and remains have been inseparable since the enactment of the federal repatriation act. Sometimes the absence has become the presence of natives, and the solar dancers await the presence of the chancers. Greene was circumspect about the investigation, as you know, and he never mentioned the death of Hildie Harridan.

Cozzie was certain that he could count on the solar dancers to support his moves against the round dancers. He named the solar dancers his constituency and was about to reveal his transnational scheme to the provost when the solar dancers arrived at the Faculty Club.

The tricky politics of native studies had changed overnight, and the patrons of solar names and manners were out. Cozzie was no more than a mass noun, and a nasty trace of intestinal gas. Round Dance, my mentor, summoned his students, and most of them were blonde, to observe a counter dance at the Faculty Club. Actually, the scene was a native sacrifice over lunch, but we could not eat because of the sickening stench. Cozzie was nervous, his shirt was stained with perspiration, and his farts were all the more deadly.

Cloud Burst and the solar dancers were always ready to accuse, and they had plenty of resentment for the stinky chicken plucker. The blonde round dancers sat in a circle around the table, and the solar dancers were perched in the four corners of the banquet room. The provost covered his nose and mouth with a napkin. He was overcome by the flatulence and bewildered by the rituals of native resentments.

Provost Greene cleared his throat several times and then asked me to introduce the students. I started out with the solar dancers, who were tucked in the four corners: Sergeant Cloud Burst, Bad Mouth, Fast Food, Touch Tone, Injun Time, Fine Print, and Token White. The solar dancers hated introductions, and one by one they ducked their heads and turned away.

Knee High, my brother, shouted Bad Mouth.

Yes, of course, in his memory.

Round Dance presented each of his students, and the solar dancers hissed at the blondes, and then returned to their corners. The provost, at first, decided not to discuss native studies with hostile students, but the solar dancers were not there for that reason anyway. They were driven by resentments and *wiindigoo* rage, of course, and they were always ready to sacrifice a fake native with chicken feathers on his sleeve.

Your names are interesting, said the provost.

Man, get bent, shouted Bad Mouth.

Please, said the provost.

My name is a vision, said Token White.

What does it mean?

Blonde bitch, shouted Bad Mouth.

Never, said Token White.

Never *indian*, shouted Bad Mouth.

Ishi is my brother, said Token White.

Yes, of course, said the provost.

Ishi was a faker, said Cozzie.

Man, shut your mouth, shouted Bad Mouth.

And your ass too, said Fast Food.

Never curse my brother, said Token White. She stopped the portable compact disc player, removed the earphones, and readied her bow. Round Dance rushed to her side and convinced her to let the insult pass. Cozzie knew he was marked, but he had no idea what had turned the solar dancers against his plan to take over native studies. He had promised that every solar dancer would graduate and receive a ceremonial blanket.

Cozzie smiled, touched the feathers on his sleeve, leaned to one side in the chair, and emitted a long, silent fart. The provost, seated next to him, almost fainted as the stink moved under the table and across the room.

FAKE INDIANS

Listen, mister provost, we got the real *indian* issues and accusations recorded right here, said Fine Print. He waved a blue examination notebook over his head. The character of the dead was on the cover. Cloud Burst beat the *wiindigoo* drum. Cozzie White Mouth is a double fake *indian*, and he never had a real shadow out there anywhere. You ask him right now, where are his traditions? Where is his community? Where is his *indian* family?

Cozzie's a faker, shouted Bad Mouth.

Fine Print stood alone at the south end of the banquet table. He opened the blue notebook, licked two fingers, turned the first few pages, and then read out loud the accusations.

The San Francisco Solar Dancers declare and decree these accusations and true issues on hand about native studies and the faker Pardone de Cozener. That stinky man, sitting right over there next to the provost, is a faker.

Stink is not a crime, said Round Dance.

Cover your mouth, said Fast Food.

Man, back to the issues, shouted Bad Mouth.

Cozzie got his skin stained for the ethnic third world, said Fine Print. So, soak him white and get him out of here tonight, and the only good thing is that he never was a blonde. Well, maybe not, but he acts like one anyway.

Custer was a blonde, said Injun Time.

Never mind, said Round Dance.

Cozzie is a fake, he never was our leader, and we demand that he be fired for stinking up the place, said Fine Print. Send him over to fart around the anthropologists. No real *indian* could stink that much all the time. His stink is white.

Cozzie lied about being an *indian* on his application to teach native studies, and that's a crime against our people, said Fine Print. He was nervous, and his voice wavered on the pitch. Cozzie refused to fill out the solar dance unitribal application form, and that's a crime against our spiritual leader.

Cloud Burst moved to each of the four directions, saluted his ruck of dancers with a drumstick, and then stood silently behind the accused at the banquet table. The provost was very nervous and turned in his chair.

Pardone de Cozener came here four winters back and told us he was a real skin, and we took him in as a brother, said Cloud Burst. Cozzie said he was a member of the mobile tribes, and when we asked him where was that, he said he was from down on the river, and when we asked him what river was that, he said way down on the *indian* river. So we did our own spiritual investigation and found out that he was a real faker.

Man, a real faker, shouted Bad Mouth.

Chickens feathers too, said Touch Tone.

Pardon me, said Provost Greene. He folded his napkin, pushed his chair back, and moved to the other side of the banquet table, away from the flatulence of the chicken plucker. What does it mean to be a fake *indian* in native studies?

Shit, man, shouted Bad Mouth. She frowned and pounded her feet on the carpet. Cloud Burst picked up the beat on the drum and the solar dancers chanted the words, fake, fuck, faker. Even the circle of blonde round dancers was moved by the beat.

Miss Bad Mouth, the very word *indian*, it seems to me, is an invention, and to assert that a person is a fake *indian*, thus a fake invention, is a tautology, said the provost. Therefore, such a person could be the opposite of the fake or invented *indian*, in the sense that double negatives serve as a positive.

Call me a double faker, said Cozzie.

Right on, shouted Bad Mouth.

We are the fake *indians* of the mobile nation, and more than that is a secret the elders told me never to mention, said Cozzie. The word may be an invention, but my secret union with the traditional mobile elders is not.

Cloud Burst beat the drum hard and fast, and the solar dancers burst into wild laughter. Fast Food bounced in the corner. Then he lighted another black cigar and spread his giant white feet on the end of the banquet table. Injun Time beat the table with his hands. The provost and the blondes, however, did not seem to grasp the irony, or how that eternal frown of the solar dancers could turn so quickly to a moment of singular pleasure. Actually, a solar dance sense of irony was a wicked breach of humor by resentment.

Cozzie lied, he's no *indian*, said Fast Food. Our spiritual investigators found no record of his enrollment in a recognized tribe, and that means he could never own a casino. Cozzie is a white man, nothing more, and he has no right to teach native studies.

Shit, man, flush the faker, shouted Bad Mouth.

Federal enrollment and recognition are white records, said Cozzie. So, how dare you curse my sacred identity only because the mobile tribe is not mentioned in white records?

What is your sacred name? shouted Bad Mouth.

Sacred names are secret, said Cozzie.

Shit, man, secret nothing.

Fake name, fake secrets, said Fine Print.

Cozzie must be removed like a white man from a reservation, because he's a fake *indian* and because he lied on his application for the job in native studies, said Fast Food. The solar dancers will never listen to him again.

Dirty Old Egg Suckin' Dog. . . .

Mister Fast Food, you must be aware of the law and university policy that race cannot, and must not, be used as a factor for any reason in either hiring or termination, said the provost.

Hires but no racial fires, shouted Bad Mouth.

That's a white catch, said Touch Tone.

Burn his ass, said Injun Time.

Please, not here, said Token White.

Round Dance surprised everyone but me when he disagreed with the solar dancers and defended Pardone de Cozener, the very person who tried to drive my mentor out of native studies. Once exposed as a fake, the chicken plucker lost forever his authority in native studies. Cozzie, my mentor said, made a better fool than an enemy, a perfect solar dance scapegoat.

Cozzie is a clown, and native studies needs a recognized fool to survive, said Round Dance. Tricksters and clowns loosen the sleeves of our visions, and, based on the tradition of native clowns, his invention as an *indian* better serves the magic moments of a scapegoat.

What traditions? asked Fine Print.

Round dance shit, shouted Bad Mouth.

Right, then we are all invented *indians*, marching in the best translations around the world, said Round Dance. The distance between a fake *indian* and the sacred is in the translation, the tricky scenes of clowns and scapegoats. So, we dare not turn against our names in translations or we might lose our balance as *indians*, fake or otherwise.

You make a good point, said the provost.

Shit, man, shouted Bad Mouth.

More, more, chanted the circle of blondes.

The sacred denies the comic because only clowns run with the sacred and silence, and clowns are their very best in translation, said Round Dance.

Ira Hayes. . . .

Man, that's white talk, shouted Bad Mouth.

Silence would end our inventions, and clowns keep that great wheel of *indian* dreams turning, turning, turning. We dare not give ourselves to that hush of the sacred, or native studies would dissolve forever in silence, said Round Dance. Natives and nature have no silence, he said, and turned to the blondes.

Man, silence the blondes, shouted Bad Mouth.

Round dance medicine, said Fine Print.

Never mind, said Injun Time.

Silence not a good mind, said the provost.

Cozzie White Mouth is our best clown for the moment in native studies, said Round Dance. Cloud Burst and the solar dancers are the victims, the round dancers are the erotic visionaries, and our own stinky chicken plucker is the perfect clown and scapegoat. Now that, my friends, creates the sacred in native studies.

Bad Mouth, however, could not be distracted from her wicked mission of resentments. She shivered on the round dance roost in the west, at the far end of the banquet room, and shouted out the other charges against Cozzie White Mouth. Cloud Burst, in turn, beat the faces on the *wiindigoo* drum.

FOWL HOUSE

Cozzie White Mouth never did nothing for *indians,* not even being one, shouted Bad Mouth. When he first came here he started a business that made *indians* look stupid.

You know it, said Injun Time.

Cozzie owns the Paraday Chicken Pluck Center on Telegraph Avenue, and he clucks on about it every day. No real *indian* would pluck the ass of a chicken, no matter what, and wear the feathers on his sleeve, shouted Bad Mouth.

Chicken molester, said Fine Print.

Free plucks for natives, said Cozzie.

Pardone de Cozener was indicted on three counts of sexual molestation of two brown pullets and a white rooster and convicted in the South Dakota Swine and Fowl Court. The ethnic emissaries reported that he was sentenced to six months hard labor at the state chicken ranch, but the judge suspended the sentence on the condition that he leave the state forever.

Cozzie took cover on several reservations, the ones that he had mapped, and then he decided to study law. Several years later he was teaching courses in native studies, and, with a strange partner, established the Paraday Chicken Pluck Center.

Mannie Medicine, a native parolee, started the first inflatable blonde rental service near the Flashback Casino on the White Earth Reservation in Minnesota. Every week hundreds of natives leased balloon blondes to ride next to them in their pickup trucks. Mannie made more money than he could count, and so he turned to roulette to win a fortune and leave the reservation, but he lost, of course, and to cover his debts sold franchise rights to blondes on other native reservations. The rights were fraudulent, and, at the same time, rumors spread that his blondes were the cause of a casino crotch rash. He was convicted of trickery in a tribal court and ordered to leave the reservation. Naturally, he moved to California.

Man, double fake *indians,* shouted Bad Mouth

Cozzie the chicken plucker, said Fine Print.

Mannie the blonde fucker, said Touch Tone.

Cozzie met Mannie and they shared the same storefront for several months on Telegraph Avenue. Cozzie provided chickens to pluck and feathers to cache. Mannie leased statuesque, inflatable blondes by the day or by the hour in booths at the back of the store. The first dummies he leased on the reservation were ungainly. He told me they were made in Romania. The new blondes, as you know, were designed by expatriates and manufactured with real hair in China.

General Custer was a blonde, said Mannie. My blondes are invented, blondes are always invented, just like *indians*, but my new inflatable mannequins promise much more pleasure, and you can choose from a wide range of body sizes and skin colors.

Cozzie and Mannie advertised their union of perverse services in booths at the back of the store, a free pluck or a blonde mannequin for an hour at a time. They hired a round dance blonde to hand out brochures on the campus:

Pluck a Chicken

Pinch a Blonde

at the

Paraday Chicken Pluck

Good Times Away from Time

Everyday is a Paraday

Cozzie told me that paraday plucks are utopian, a plucked feather has no time, love, or hate. Chicken plucks are pure, absolute pleasures and a tease of separation and culture. He got his start with chickens at cocking mains in backyards and abandoned houses near Jack London Square in Oakland. I could barely think of anything else, he said, when the great cocks were in town, the sacred Shawlnecks and Baltimore Topknots.

He became a breeder and soon had his own champion cocks, and that was the start of his chicken pluck service. Cozzie constructed cock pens and pullet pillories in private booths, and overnight the store was filled with chicken pluckers. Faculty and students came by the hundreds to pluck, pluck, pluck white feathers hour after hour from the plump rumps of chickens, cluck, cluck, cluck. The private booths were named after five varieties of domestic chickens.

Cozzie lectured on casino politics and sovereignty in native studies by day and cozied his chickens at night. Mannie and Cozzie shared the same store, but their clients were seldom the same. The pluckers were moved by more distinct passions and rarely ever leased a blonde. Mostly men leased the blondes, and more women than men plucked chickens. Their services were very profitable for several years, and then, as they prepared to expand in several other communities, an earthquake crushed the mannequins and liberated most of the chickens. Cozzie rebuilt his cock pens and pillories, but in a separate store. Mannie moved across the street next to the bookstore. He expanded his services, leased erotic costumes and other mannequins of men, women, and children, and sold a new herbal cigar. Mannie boasted that his aromatic *Indian Highs* cured colds, cancer, sudden rashes, and certainty.

Cozzie runs a fowl house, shouted Bad Mouth.

You should know, said Round Dance.

Bad Mouth was the first in line for the free pluck, but when she shouted the cock turned around and pecked two holes in the back of her hand. Cozzie and his chickens have been on her solar dance list of resentments ever since.

Cozzie invited the pluckers to write a few words about their experiences with chickens. The leatherbound book was on a table near the entrance of the Paraday Chicken Pluck. Pictures of several rooster breeds and cock fighters were mounted on the walls and displayed in the windows. Professors, lawyers, carpenters, poets, librarians, philosophers, students, retired farmers, and others wrote their thoughts in the book. The pluckers, as you know, were partial to certain breeds of chickens. These notes were copied from the book of chicken pluck confessions.

Cornish Plucker: Pluck the hackles and saddles, and with the feathers make me a headdress the hawks would admire on the road, wrote a retired philosophy professor who plucked twice a week in a private booth.

Plymouth Rock Plucker: My culture is a wild chicken the world would love to pluck, pluck, pluck, wrote a graduate student in anthropology. My chance to touch a chicken is mythic, my feathers are secret, and we soar in magical flight to our favorite nests in the mountains.

New Hampshire Plucker: That woman of mine saved your necks from the axe, but now she's gone, buried in chicken shit out back on the farm, and here we are, alone in a private booth, wrote a retired farmer. Cozzie noted that he never really plucked but grabbed three chickens at a time by the short legs and bounced them up and down in the booth until white chicken shit covered his wrists.

Dorking Plucker: God is a chicken feather, wrote a librarian who always wore a black feathered coat. Feathers are my magic, my dance, my natural ruffle, and the hackles touch my inner chicken, cluck, cluck, cluck.

Rhode Island Red Plucker: I am not a chicken plucker, I am the chicken plucker's daughter, wrote a tiny woman who clucked back at the chickens. I am only plucking chickens until the chicken plucker comes. She did more clucking than plucking in a private booth.

LONESOME STUDIES

Provost Greene cleared his throat several times and then beat the table with his shoe to command the attention of the solar dancers and the faculty. He boldly announced that an official investigation of native studies revealed bloodline resentments and irreconcilable administrative problems. In other words, native studies is over the side without an academic mission, irrecoverable, said the provost. Namely, there are four investigative points of summary.

First, it has been revealed that native studies records seven times the campus rate of independent study course credit, said the provost. Native students, our investigators observed, have earned several semesters of credit for summer experience at home on the reservation, and nothing more. Personal, native anecdotes are not an academic course.

Second, an audit and investigation revealed that two state minivans were driven to reservations and used in *indian* protests without authorization. The students used university credit cards to charge more than six hundred dollars in gasoline and fast food, said the provost. Recently, an *indian* student testified that he was lonesome for his grandmother and drove a university vehicle to the Pine Ridge Reservation in South Dakota. Our auditors pointed out, however, that the minivan was used in the production of the motion picture, *Dances With Wolves*.

Shit, man, tradition, shouted Bad Mouth.

Did you like the movie? asked Fine Print.

Fast Food moved to the chair next to the provost, lighted a black cigar, and blew smoke in his face. The aromatic smoke, however, seemed to negate the stink of Cozzie. The provost smiled and continued his administrative indictments.

Third, the *indian* students and solar dancers charged twelve times more long-distance telephone calls, amounting to several thousand dollars a semester, than any other department on the university campus, said the provost. Dependence on the oral tradition is no longer an acceptable explanation for so many expensive long-distance calls. For instance, last semester someone made nineteen calls to the Pine Ridge Reservation, thirteen calls to the Bad River Reservation, five very expensive conference calls to Hindustan, two calls to Saskatchewan, and seven calls to the People's Republic of China.

Shit, man, too much, shouted Bad Mouth.

Talk is natural, said Fast Food.

Moderation is the word, said the provost.

Telephones are a tease, said Touch Tone. Naturally, we have sovereign rights to the oral tradition, so you can understand that we have more to say about the sacred than a white man does. Yes, and what about my calls to the clerk of court in Saskatchewan?

Green, Green Grass of Home. . . .

Fourth, seventeen *indian* students charged to the university the total cost of their summer vacation back home to reservations. Such travel is not authorized, and in any case the amount far exceeded the total travel allowance of native studies. Lonesome home leave and travel is not academic and is not covered by the university.

The faculty and students of native studies have violated many times over every fiscal policy, said the provost. Consequently,

after repeated notices and reprimands for these serious violations, the faculty senate has decided to terminate native studies
at the end of this academic year. Therefore, you may, as sched-
uled, conduct the terminal native studies commencement this
summer in the Mather Redwood Grove.

"This story is no good, I'm beginning almost to believe it,"
wrote Samuel Beckett in *The Unnamable*. "But let us see how it
is supposed to end, that will sober me. The trouble is I forget
how it goes on. But did I ever know?"

HOLY DECADENCE

Round Dance circled
the microphone
as he presented
honorary degrees to
Ishi and Tulip Browne.
The University of California
is honored to bestow
upon you many chancers,
in spirit, stolen blankets,
and presentiments,
the degree,
doctor of humane letters,
honoris causa.

BLANKET RUINS

The Golden Gate Bridge put to sea on the pacific fog, and evermore the native clowns round the mast to tease the ghosts, forestays on the rise in stories, over the haunted waves, cautious over the *wiindigoo* waves, over the concrete bunkers, traces of the solar dance, the turtles and tricksters of the last memories in the stone, and native visions move with the crows above the earth, above the reach of winter in the trees, the wind, the ocean creases, the sudden crests and break of voices, and mighty natives dance roundabout in stories to hear the rush of words over every face of creation.

The ethnic emissaries seldom comment, as you know, on my stories. Surely, you were never pleased with wild, imagistic scenes. The metaphors of creation are at the very heart of native stories, but the narrative cuts of causation and motivation are much easier to represent as realism to readers. Likewise, objective, authentic scenes and linear action are more important in the collection and evaluation of ethnic intelligence. The emissaries favor the fiction of manners, the bait of victimry, and resist the visionary.

There are gestures on the other side of reason here, the sounds of creation in the stone, crows on the rise of summer, the shimmer of our many faces in the ocean haze, but the lure, attitude, ideology, objective action, motivation, and causation matter more than visions and transmotion to the ethnic emissaries.

I write to the ethnic emissaries, as you know, and you know me in a virtual presence. You read me here and never respond to the obvious. You resist visions and the conversions of the tricksters, but not my stories about natives. Native tricksters are never motivated, as you know, and yet they are the very tease of creation, motion, and action. The native trickster is in every word, no matter the manner, reason, translation, narrative style, or interpretation. The trickster is forever at the touch and go of shadows and transmotion in native stories.

You are the emissaries, my readers, not my conscience, but we find a tricky solace in the silent, fugitive pose of words on a computer monitor. By this silence have my stories been turned into the myths of causality and representation, or the ceremonial power of a sand painting? The sacred figures of pollen and sand are ephemeral, and so are the metaphors of creation stories. The intimations of healers are elusive, and my words are shadows, a virtual presence, more pollen and sand than objective representations. My emissaries, you are the barren masks, erased at the end of each ethnic document. My stories are virtual, an elusive native presence.

Native stories endure, but the listeners and readers are only chances in a scene, a trace in a portrait of a trickster. The emissaries are dead voices on the monitor, and my stories go on, they must go on, in the silence and shadow of words, or so it seems in the world of native chancers. How much do we simulate at the crossover of sound and scripture the words to name our presence?

The emissaries erase my stories and virtual presence at the end of their ethnic intelligence reports. They determine the reason and manner of every word and scene, the turn of crows, creases of wind, mighty moans, cracks in ice and stone, and the blue lightning. You read this, as you know, and, of course, you do know my scenes.

The morning ghosts were on the rise over the ocean waves, and later, the great white clouds covered San Francisco Bay. The fog teased the spires, moved by wisps, streams, and chunks, and shrouded the Phoebe Apperson Hearst Museum of Anthropology, the Faculty Club, Senior Hall, and then rushed over the narrow trails of Strawberry Canyon. The hungry fog lingered in the boughs of the Mather Redwood Grove.

Stephen Tyng Mather might have been pleased that natives held their commencement in the giant redwoods that he once protected and celebrated. Mather graduated, as you know, from the University of California three generations earlier, made a fortune in borax, and then, as the assistant to the secretary of the interior, he established the National Park Service. Mather was not an advocate of native sovereignty, but he stood by the evergreens, the native rights of natural scenes, and blocked the timber barons and butchers of the redwoods. The manes shimmered on the mighty boughs, and the solar dancers haunted the redwoods in his name.

The redwoods dance, said Token White.

Shit, man, this is spooky, shouted Bad Mouth.

This be graduation, said Fine Print.

Shoot the fakes and faculty, said Fast Food.

Kill Cozzie, shouted Bad Mouth.

Mannie too, said Injun Time.

Shit, man, he's a woman, shouted Bad Mouth.

Bad Mouth learned that she would not receive a blanket, a singular native token of academic achievement, because she had failed two courses and was eight credits short of the requirements for a degree. So, never to be denied by necessity, she stole the whole bundle of *indian* blankets from the storage area and gave one to each of the solar dancers.

Token White, outraged by the theft, told me that she marked each blanket with the blue character of death. She was certain the solar dancers would return the blankets out of fear once they saw the *wiindigoo* character, the same one that marked the provost and bone lovers for sacrifice. She was mistaken, the

solar dancers wore the blankets later at the graduation ceremony. Pendleton wool blankets with *indian* designs, such as
morning star, spider woman, turtle, chief eagle, mother earth,
and spirit quest, were ordered for each graduate in native
studies, but only one, a commemoration of spider woman,
could be found that afternoon in the redwood grove.

Token White was the only solar dancer who ever graduated, and, as you know, she earned honors for her senior
thesis on "The Art of Native Archery." The solar dancers were
eager to use her as an archer, but they resented her color, tal-
ents, and success as a student in native studies.

Flushed from the Bathroom of your Heart. . . .

Fast Food traced with his thick thumbnail the soft grain in
the wooden bench at the back of the arena. Bored, he raised
tiny curves and slivers of redwood and sucked on a thin, black,
aromatic cigar. His smoky breath lasted in the moist air, deadly.

Injun Time was stimulated by the smoke. He too leaned
back on the bench and lighted an aromatic *Indian High* cigar.
He studied the waves of smoke, the thin rise of poison into the
boughs of the redwoods. Later he told me that a shaker marriage came to mind, white and glorious, and he rang the hand-
bells on the run in great circles.

The Stellar's Jays shouted at the solar dancers.

Injun Time pictured solar dancers in the smoke and became
drowsy. He closed his eyes and the lighted cigar slipped out of
his fingers and rolled down his chest. Minutes later his white
nylon jacket was ablaze. His braided black hair sizzled, and
his face shriveled in the flames as he threw his jacket on the
ground. The fire spread in the dry brush at the side of the road.

Bad Mouth seized the last *indian* blanket, the bright blue spider woman, and covered his head to save his hair. Great clouds of smoke arose in the canyon and moved with the fog.

Injun Time cursed *Indian High* cigars as the solar dancers carried him out of the redwoods. Cloud Burst loaded him into the back of his minivan. Injun Time smoldered, a fleshy stench, as they raced down the canyon. The smoke clouded the windows. The caravan of solar dancers arrived at the hospital about the same time the emergency vehicles reached the blaze in the redwoods.

Touch Tone told me the solar dancers cursed everyone for the cigar fire. Bad Mouth blamed Mannie Medicine for the fire because he rolled and sold the aromatic *Indian High* cigars at his store. She was a crone of resentments and had no sense of chance, irony, or responsibility.

Token White was left behind, the only solar dancer present for the start of the graduation ceremonies that afternoon. The fire was contained in a few minutes, and the commencement proceeded as planned. Round Dance, my mentor, was eager to take advantage of the absence of the solar dancers, so he moved the ceremonies ahead without delay.

Bad Mouth, meanwhile, cursed the nurses and doctors at the hospital for their service and delay. She marched into the emergency room and shouted that the solar dancers would send *wiindigoo* demons to haunt the hospital if the doctors did not save Injun Time. Then, once the solar dancers learned that he would recover from the burns, they turned their hatred toward Token White. Fine Print told me they cursed her for not being at the hospital and for being the only one to graduate.

Man, she's white, shouted Bad Mouth.

Token White's no dancer, said Touch Tone.

She's a witch, said Fine Print.

Cloud Burst beat the faces on the *wiindigoo* drum and the sound thundered in the hospital corridors. Fast Food danced to the beat, and the smack of his huge white feet aroused the nurses. Fine Print told me that patients came out of their rooms, many of them towing medicine carts, and danced in their gowns. The solar dancers reached out to heal the sick, and, at the same time, they cursed the healers.

DOCTOR ISHI

Tulip Browne was an agent of escape distances. She waited at the side of the arena to evade conversations with the round dancers, and to duck the stink of Cozzie White Mouth. Provost Greene and my mentor had invited her to receive an honorary degree and to deliver the commencement lecture. The mighty redwood trees were specters in the haze, and the manes were in the boughs.

She mounted the stage and uncovered a copper windmill on the table next to the lectern. The miniature blades whirred on the slightest breeze, a natural balance, and the meditative whisper of the blades reached to the back rows of the arena in the Mather Redwood Grove.

Tulip touched the microphone, and the rush of sound overcame the mellow whir of the windmills. She paid tribute to her niece, the elevator shaman, but to no one else, and then, with no introduction, she boldly announced that there were two natural systems of native survivance. The students and parents might have heard the word surveillance instead of survivance, because they leaned closer to hear the secrets of a private investigator.

Gregory Bateson, she said, writes in *Mind and Nature* that "there are typically two energetic systems in interdependence: one is the system that uses its energy to open or close the faucet or gate or relay; the other is the system whose energy flows through the faucet or gate when it is open."

Natives created a natural sense of presence on the move, and thereby opened the gates of imagination and a visionary survivance, said Tulip. Naturally, the rest of the world has been flowing through our stories ever since. Natives are forever praised and studied for their secrets, ceremonies, cultures, and entire academic systems are generated in the names of natives.

Mother earth hearsay, said Round Dance.

Never mind, said Conk.

Ishi, consider that one name and you might understand the meaning and interdependence of these two systems, she told the audience. Ishi has no other name but the reaction of an institution, the discovery, academic nomination, and, at last, the liberation of a character in a world of chance and contingency.

Ishi is my brother, said Token White.

Cloud Burst must have heard her voice on the beat, because he turned from the *wiindigoo* drum and told his nasty ruck to leave the hospital and head for the minivan. Minutes later, moved by hatred and resentments, the solar dancers marched into the back of the arena, unaware of the blue *wiindigoo* character of the dead on the stolen blankets over their shoulders.

Bad Mouth sneered and shouted at a mongrel tied to a tree. Fast Food stretched his huge white feet out in the center aisle and wagged his toes. The other solar dancers were perched on the redwood benches in the back rows.

I Still Miss Someone. . . .

Ishi is here today, in the high haze of these mighty trees, said Tulip. She pointed to the back rows and announced the names of the solar dancers, one by one, over the meditative whir of the windmill, Cloud Burst, Bad Mouth, Fast Food, Touch Tone, and Fine Print. Injun Time is in the hospital, or he would be here. Token White was not named in the ruck, because she was seated in the first row ready to receive her degree, and with honors. The solar dancers are here, and they have decided to return the stolen blankets, said Tulip. The parents and students turned in silence.

This is my blanket, shouted Bad Mouth.

My mother earth, said Touch Tone.

Ishi is here with his many admirers, Alfred Kroeber, Phoebe Apperson Hearst, Edward Sapir, Thomas Waterman, and Saxton Pope, to receive with me the distinction of an honorary degree, doctor of humane letters, *honoris causa.*

Ishi is always here, said Token White.

Alfred Kroeber is here, said Tulip.

Knee High is here, shouted Bad Mouth.

Edward Sapir is here, said Round Dance.

Saxton Pope, shouted Token White.

Phoebe Apperson Hearst, said Cozzie.

Snow Boy, shouted Bad Mouth.

Louis Riel is here, said Touch Tone.

Ira Hayes, said Token White.

Pontius Booker, said Ransom Greene.

Ruby Blue Welcome, said Cozzie.

Pocahontas is here, said Conk Browne.

John Rolfe again, said Round Dance.

Not a chance, shouted Bad Mouth.

John Martin Peterson, said Cloud Burst.

Four Skins is here, said Round Dance.

Man, stop this shit, shouted Bad Mouth. She paced back and forth in the back rows of the arena. Whenever she waved her arms and shouted the blanket dropped to the ground. She stumbled twice in the middle of shouts. The blondes in the front rows turned and snickered. Bad Mouth twice tried to shout, my brother is not here.

Round Dance circled the microphone as he presented honorary degrees to Ishi and Tulip Browne. The University of California is honored to bestow upon you many chancers, in a tricky native spirit, stolen blankets, and presentiments, the degree, doctor of humane letters, *honoris causa.*

My brother is here, said Token White.

He's a faker, said Fast Food.

Ishi's not an *indian,* shouted Bad Mouth.

Ishi is Yahi, said Round Dance.

Man, you know nothing, shouted Bad Mouth.

Alfred Kroeber moved to the lectern, a gentle man with a worried heart and a very distant voice. He studied the windmill for a few minutes and then told the audience that Ishi, his friend, was the most patient man he ever knew. I mean he had mastered the philosophy of patience.

Ishi sold out to a museum, shouted Bad Mouth. She marched down the center aisle towing a stolen graduation blanket. Kroeber, man, you made him an *indian*, because he can't even prove he's from anywhere.

Saxton Pope, the medical doctor and master of bows and arrows, turned the microphone to the side and leaned on the lectern. Ishi, he said, looked upon us as sophisticated children, smart but not wise. His voice was steady and strong. We knew many things, and much that was false. Ishi knew nature, which is always true. His soul was that of a child, his mind that of a philosopher.

Evelybody hoppy, said Ishi.

Yes, we are hoppy, said Token White.

Nobody was ever hoppy, man, because you need a white man to come alive, shouted Bad Mouth. Kroeber made you a museum boy, and now you don't even have a reservation.

GHOST DANCE

Cozzie White Mouth wore a white cotton suit, floral print tie, a vest with bright red stripes, and a blue academic robe decorated with seventeen white stars, one for each of the graduates. He mounted the stage by half steps, out of breath, and, as usual, farted in motion, an eternal trace of his creation. The thick robe absorbed most of the stink, but we were never sure and abandoned the stage. Cozzie was determined, once again, to announce the names of the graduates, and, at a safe distance, my mentor conferred the actual degrees on the students.

My brother is here, said Token White.

My sister is here, said Conk.

Evelybody gets a degree, said Cozzie.

Flag Day was one of the nicknames he earned at graduation ceremonies. Cozzie delivered the same lecture every year
to honor the flag. Yes, the stars and stripes. Many students and
parents who otherwise might have been patriotic protested
that he actually debased the flag by his suit and inane comments on the colors, red, white, and blue.

Round Dance and the provost had encouraged him to create
a native sense of presence in his presentation at the last graduation ceremony. The stories of the flag, however, were mundane, barely tricky enough to hold the attention of the students.

George Washington told a few lies in his time, but the story
of the flag is true, said Cozzie White Mouth. George once
noticed that an *indian* he met on the road wore a blue shirt
with white stars, and the sleeves were decorated with red and
white ribbons. He was told that the white stars were the story
marks of the many white men the warrior had killed in the
revolution. George was an honest man and assumed the very
best of sides, but he was mistaken that summer, because, you
see, the *indian* was not a patriot of the new nation, he was a
royalist. The Continental Congress heard the story of a native
patriot and created a flag of thirteen stripes, white between
red bands like *indian* ribbons, and stars in the blue.

Man, he stole our shirt, shouted Bad Mouth.

Our blankets are flags, said Fine Print.

George asked his wife to create the first flag, a new union of
thirteen states. The white stars on a blue background were
morning stars, the visions and story marks of the ghost dance.

This flag of a new nation was an *indian* story, a constellation of visions, and my robe is a morning star, a celebration of that story, said Cozzie White Mouth.

> my children
> my children
> I wear the morning star on my head
> I wear the morning star on my head
> I show it to my children
> I show it to my children
> says the father
> says the father

Cozzie announced seventeen graduates in the redwood grove that afternoon. The graduates were praised by everyone but the solar dancers, who lurked at the back of the arena. Token White was the only student to earn honors, so she was named to receive the one blanket that had not been stolen by the solar dancers. Round Dance laid the spider woman blanket over her shoulder and conferred a bachelor's degree.

Ira Hayes. . . .

Injun Time is in the hospital, and he earned this blanket, said Token White. This is the spider woman blanket that smothered the blaze and saved his braids. She folded the blanket, placed it on the stage, and asked me to deliver it to the hospital.

Evelybody hoppy, mocked Mannie Medicine.

Ishi is my brother, said Token White.

Honoree hoppy, hoppy, said Mannie.

Never mock my brother, said Token White.

Shit, man, evelybody white on stage, shouted Bad Mouth. She waved her hands in a rage and scared the mongrels in the back rows of the arena. Ishi, man, he never was no *indian,* she shouted, he was cooked up by anthropologists. She threw pinecones and stones at the stage.

Cozzie told Mannie to entertain the students and parents with his tricky, transformational stories while the hors d'oeuvres were being prepared for the reception. The solar dancers were there for the food and resentments.

Mannie burned our brother, shouted Bad Mouth.

Now you die, said Fine Print.

Mannie threw some of the stones back at the solar dancers and mocked their separatist moves. He pranced alone onstage and seemed to be more secure with an audience than he was in his own store, but taunting the solar dancers was never a wise move. They were naturals at cruel revenge, as you know, and gruesome sacrifice. Mannie was cursed forever by the solar dancers because he had sold aromatic *Indian High* cigars to Injun Time.

Mannie had erected a curtain onstage to hide his costumes and conversions. He first wore long black braids, bound with leather and bright ribbons, and pitched his voice to morose *indian* traditions, in the manner of Clyde Bellecourt and Dennis Banks of the American Indian Movement. Later he donned an enormous blond wig and wore a red cocktail dress with silver sequins. Mannie danced, raised his dress, and pretended to show his crotch, but he revealed nothing more than a transparent plastic teaser stuffed with steel wool, a simulation of pubic hair. Then he wore a great robe made of chicken feathers. Paraday Pluck was written in dark hackles on the back.

Shit, man, pluck that freak, shouted Bad Mouth.

Stand by the pluckers, said Cozzie. This is chancer time at our last commencement. So, the provost must never misremember what the university once had in native studies, the foundational cultures and histories of this great nation.

Native chancer time, said Mannie. He circled the stage with his hands raised and then ducked behind the curtain. He shouted the names of many native chancers, Pocahontas, Ishi, Riel, Geronimo, Hayes, Crazy Horse, and Sitting Bull. Then, in an eerie tease at the curtain, he chanted the names of Pontius Booker, Snow Boy, Hildie Harridan, Blue Welcome, and last but not least, Four Skins.

Four Skins won the favor of the audience. The faculty and students stood to honor the sacred name, and parents who had graduated decades earlier remembered the great stories of the wise and wicked hand puppet at native commencements. Truly, he was the most memorable chancer on campus.

Graduates, parents, friends, and faculty, a warm hand for the chancer Four Skins, said Cozzie. The solar dancers were in a rage at the back of the arena, but the audience saluted the resurrection of the memorable hand puppet who had vanished on campus, leaving only his giant penis in a museum case.

Mannie moved backwards out of the curtain and walked to the center of the stage. Four Skins, the younger, was hidden beneath his chicken feather robe. He teased the audience with hand gestures and then slowly uncovered the bright, erect head of Four Skins.

The audience was ecstatic at the sight of the chancer. Students and their parents bounced in wild circles, and many students ran down the aisles and threw their gowns onstage.

Provost Greene was moved to tears by the show of affection for a mere hand puppet, but he never wavered on his notice of the last commencement.

Four Skins the chancer turned an erotic smile and bowed to the audience, a natural move in the hands of Mannie Medicine. Many students and their parents mimicked the moves of Four Skins. When he moved, they moved in the same manner, a mirror gesture, and in that way the audience became the very embodiment of the chancer.

Four Skins, the younger, had the erotic wit of the elder puppet but the actual mind of a cyborg. Blue Welcome had her way with the original puppet, and she told his stories in a bold ventriloquial voice. Mannie, on the other hand, thrust his fingers into the body of the puppet, but not to directly move his mouth. Rather, he fitted his hand into an electronic glove and the puppet moved in virtual reality. Four Skins was wired to move by gesture, and he repeated more than a hundred stories, most of them about the sex lives of the rich, the academic, and the scandalous on campus.

Four Skins, for instance, told erotic stories about how he beat out three terriers to be with his lover, Ruby Blue Welcome. Snow Boy, on the other hand, was a wild bone man who aroused the jealousy of the puppet. Four Skins, the younger, also told gruesome stories about how the provost had vanished on his merry way to the Faculty Club. The stories were true, as you know, but incredible to the audience. The puppet went on to surprise everyone with a witty story about how the blankets were stolen by the solar dancers.

Man, these are *indian* flags, said Fast Food.

Four Skins continued his indictments of thievery, debauchery, witchery, and grade forgery. He had the stories right, and the solar dancers were furious. They refused to give up the blankets and protested that the provost must intervene to protect their rights.

Four Skins is a liar, said Touch Tone.

Man, that geek is dead, shouted Bad Mouth.

No puppet is a chancer, said Fast Food.

Four Skins announced that the twice stolen bones of his sister were at the Azhetaa Center in Half Moon Bay. Pocahontas is my chancer, and the solar dancers buried her sweet bones on the beach, shouted Four Skins.

Pocahontas wandered out of the redwoods at the side of the stage. She winked at the puppet, and then bowed to her sister. You see, she said, you heard my stories on the elevator, and now we come together as chancers.

Were you stolen? asked Conk.

Buried thrice by chance, said Pocahontas.

How many chancers are here for the last native commencement? asked Four Skins. Slowly, one by one, chancers raised their hands in the arena. Actually, we were astounded that there were so many. Most of the elders in the audience were chancers. Round Dance was touched by a great loneliness for his parents and grandparents. My father and grandmother were there. They raised their hands and teased me.

Fine Print decided to terminate the puppet, chancer or not, right in front of the students, parents, and faculty. He nocked the string of his long bow and lighted a gasoline soaked arrow. The flaming arrow creased the moist air over the heads of the students and parents and struck the puppet master in the thigh. The arrow set his robe afire.

Mannie and Four Skins were caught in a blaze of chicken feathers. He protected the puppet as the feathers crackled and the fire spread to his blond wig. Token White rushed to the stage and threw spider woman, the only free graduation blanket, over Mannie and Four Skins.

Four Skins continued his stories under spider woman, the very same blanket that had smothered human blazes in the redwood grove. Cozzie was there minutes later to douse the smoky ruins with bottled water. The putrid smell of burned chicken feathers blended with other stinks onstage.

Mannie was on his back, in the ruins of his coat, worried that he would never become a chancer in chicken feathers. Ishi dragged him out of his feathers, tore his trousers open, and gently turned the arrow. Cozzie was pained and moaned in sympathy. Ishi removed the arrow, and blood slowly oozed from the shallow wound on his hairy white thigh.

Saxton Pope first examined the arrow, the turn of the shaft, the four dove feathers, and then turned to the wounded puppet master on the stage. He teased the patient about his feathers and puppets as he cleaned the wound with water and whiskey. Alfred Kroeber, at his side, tore his white shirt apart to make bandages. Mannie was treated and bound by three great chancers.

We are together again, said Token White.

Not a chance, shouted Bad Mouth.

Token White hated the elder hand puppet, as you know, but that afternoon she was rather touched by the witty stories of the chancer. Four Skins was rescued from the blaze and thrown on the lectern. She raised his head and held his hand as he told stories about solar dancers and cyborgs. Four Skins leaned closer to the microphone. That Bad Mouth, he said, had nasty sex with her miniature brother, and now she masturbates over his bones, but the evildoers never had a chance, never a chancer. Cloud Burst had sex with his mother and told me that she was none other than Sirius the Dog Star in the constellation Canis Major.

Four Skins, the elder, and the chancer had no sense of the risk and shock of their stories. The first puppet was kidnapped, tortured, and cremated, as you know, and his penis was traded as an amulet on campus. Four Skins, the new chancer, taunted and mocked, to his peril, the ruck of solar dancers.

Cloud Burst was at the end of his vision, a terminal wrath, as he beat the faces on the *wiindigoo* drum. The beat was hard but the sound was muted in the redwoods at the back of the arena. Slowly, the solar dancers circled the drum, shrouded in stolen blankets that were marked with the character of the dead. They shivered, one by one on the beat, and moaned with resentments.

Mannie hobbled to the lectern, hugged his mouthy puppet, and thanked the students and parents for their trust, humor, and glory. At that very mawkish moment, several arrows hit the lectern, tore the curtain, and bounced on stage. Fine Print, who never became a serious, meditative archer, shot as many arrows as he could nock, some two and three at a time, toward the stage. Yet, the primitive barrage of arrows missed the round dancers. Only two chancers were struck by the arrows. Four

Skins was wounded in the chest, at the very heart of his digital memory, but the wound was minor, he lost seven stories about chancers in the movies, *Dances With Wolves* and *Smoke Signals*. Phoebe Apperson Hearst was hit in the crotch, but the arrow cut straight through her thick gown and missed her fleshy parts.

Cloud Burst beat the *wiindigoo* drum harder and the solar dancers shouted and cursed the blondes, the round dancers, and the faculty. The students and parents disregarded the taunts of the solar ruck and carried on with the reception, the very last taste of wine and hors d'oeuvres at a native studies commencement.

Fine Print was anxious, not disposed to meditation, so he considered the crude trajectory and changed his tactics. He lobbed one flaming arrow at a time toward the stage. The arrows stuck in the chairs, lectern, and floor, but several students tracked the arrows and rushed to douse the flames with water.

Fast Food told me that he wanted to be remembered as the solar dancer who burned the last commencement. He watched the arrows miss the mark and decided to cast his remembrance with gasoline siphoned from the minivan. Plastic bucket in hand, he ran down the aisle, smacking his great white feet on the cold concrete, and poured the gasoline on the stage. He moved back, lighted a black cigar, and threw the match at the lectern. The hardwood burst, the lectern crackled and hissed, and the wild sound was broadcast throughout the arena until the microphone wheezed, overcome by the intense flames. The war of the native dancers, solar and round, had been declared by the *wiindigoo*, not by erotic blondes, academic manes, or by the chancers.

Token White turned away from the blaze onstage, raised her head, and concentrated on the motion of the redwoods. Thin streams of mist rushed over the boughs, a natural wave of light. Ishi touched her hair as she shouldered a quiver of arrows. She nocked the string of her sacred Yahi bow, made of mountain juniper, and moved to the center of the arena in the Mather Redwood Grove.

The blaze was at her back, and the heat of the fire toned the grain of the bow. She closed her eyes and moved her head to one side and then the other, a meditative gesture. Sirens sounded in the distance, an emergency response to the fire on stage. Cloud Burst beat the faces on the *wiindigoo* drum, and the solar dancers circled in a trance at the back of the arena.

Fine Print raised his long bow, aimed his last arrow at his archery teacher, but he shivered, wavered, and lost his wicked concentration. Token White covered her eyes with black velvet and created the presence of the solar dancers in a vision. Actually, she did not want to see the panic and mockery of fear in their eyes. She uncovered her eyes much later, only when she heard the crash of the minivan with a fire truck and a double explosion.

Fine Print was struck dead by the first arrow, a hazel stick smoothed over heated stones. The point, flaked out of thick blue bottle glass, cut clean through his heart. He stood for several seconds with an expression of sudden, unexpected pleasure and then toppled over on his back.

Fast Food was silent, an awkward dancer in a stolen blanket. The arrow struck the *wiindigoo* character on his side, burst his heart, and came out under his arm on the other side. The point was under one arm and the feathers were under the other. He held the ends of the arrow, ran toward the redwoods, and marked the bark of a tree with his blood. He went down on his side and the arrow snapped as he turned on his back. His great white toes were erect.

Touch Tone circled the drum in a wild dance. She threw the blanket aside. The ribbons on her bright shirt moved on the breeze. She turned from the drum and danced toward Token White. The arrow stuck in her heart, but she continued to dance down the aisle to the front of the arena. Then she sat on a bench, spread the ribbons out, and lost her breath.

Bad Mouth waved the ceremonial trade axe that Fast Food had stolen from the bone museum. She shouted and cursed the blonde archer, and then she rushed down the aisle with the axe above her head. Token White raised her bow and released three arrows, one at a time. Bad Mouth was fierce, moved by demonic energy. The first arrow struck her in the chest, but only nicked her tiny, lopsided heart. The second arrow tore a hole in her stomach, and blood poured out over her thighs. The third arrow pierced her head, just above her eyes. Bad Mouth ran down the aisle, axe in hand, and into the blaze onstage. She was a wicked cinder by the time the emergency vehicles arrived at the scene.

That was my trade axe, said Phoebe Hearst.

Serves you right, said Cozzie.

Cloud Burst was in a savage heave as he beat the last faces on his *wiindigoo* drum. Token White released two thick arrows. The first stuck in the side of the drum, and created a wild vibration. The obsidian point of the second arrow pierced the side of the drum, and eerie voices escaped into the redwoods.

Cloud Burst ran to his minivan, and in his rush to escape the arrows he crashed into a fire engine on the canyon road. The first explosion was caused by a ruptured gasoline tank on the minivan, and the second explosion was a mystery. The faculty thought it was an echo, the students said explosives might have detonated in the minivan, and others worried that the second burst was the sound of the *wiindigoo* demons at the last commencement. The students burned the stolen blankets with the blue characters.

What a time this has been, said Alfred Kroeber.

Evelybody hoppy? asked Ishi.